## "We Used to Have Some Good Times Together."

Lifting a hand, Ridge trailed a finger along her cheekbone and tucked a strand of hair behind her ear. "Didn't we?"

"Yes." Sharon didn't trust herself to say more. There was a poignant drift of memories back to that time he had recalled. . . . She had built so many dreams from those innocent evenings in Ridge's company. She had wanted so much to believe he loved her that she had exaggerated every slow dance, every kiss, out of all proportion.

Long ago Sharon had stopped trying to second-guess his motives, so she didn't allow herself to wonder whether he was caught in a past memory when his calloused fingers laid themselves against the curve of her neck and the warm pressure of his mouth covered her lips. . . .

**Books by Janet Dailey**

The Great Alone
The Glory Game
The Pride of Hannah Wade
Silver Wings, Santiago Blue
Calder Born, Calder Bred
Stands a Calder Man
This Calder Range
This Calder Sky
The Best Way to Lose
For the Love of God
Foxfire Light
The Hostage Bride
The Lancaster Men
Leftover Love
Mistletoe & Holly
The Second Time
Separate Cabins
Terms of Surrender
Western Man
Nightway
Ride the Thunder
The Rogue
Touch the Wind

Published by POCKET BOOKS

# JANET DAILEY

# WESTERN MAN

POCKET BOOKS

New York   London   Toronto   Sydney   Tokyo   Singapore

POCKET BOOKS, a division of Simon & Schuster Inc.
1230 Avenue of the Americas, New York, NY 10020

Copyright © 1983 by Janbill, Ltd.

Originally published by Silhouette Books.

ISBN: 0-671-87521-3

First Pocket Books printing May 1986

10  9  8  7

Map by Ray Lundgren

POCKET and colophon are registered trademarks of
Simon & Schuster Inc.

Printed in the U.S.A.

# WESTERN
# MAN

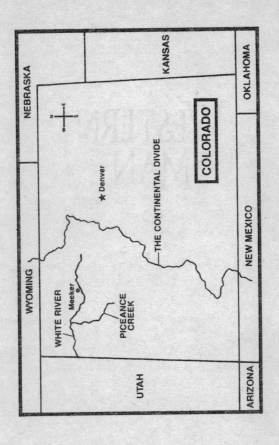

# Chapter One

The ranch-house kitchen was filled with the warm smell of chocolate chip cookies fresh from the oven. When the last cookie on the metal sheet pan joined the others cooling on the paper spread on the counter top, Sharon Powell turned to carry the sheet pan to the table where the bowl of cookie dough sat.

Her hazel-eyed glance fell on the empty chair pushed away from the table, where a half-finished glass of milk remained along with two cookies, each with a bite taken from it. Her reaction was a combination of alarm and exasperation.

"Tony?" Sharon tossed a potholder onto the table and laid the cookie sheet, hot from the oven, on to it. There was no response to her querying call, although she strained alertly to catch any sound. Muttering to herself, Sharon started out in search of the toddler. "Now I know why they call them terrible two-year-olds. I turn my back on him for two minutes and he disappears."

This time she didn't have to search far or long to

find the boy. As soon as she entered the living room, she spied him standing at the screen door, stretching a small hand to reach the latch. A wry shake of her head sent her short, toffee-colored ponytail swaying.

"Come on, Tony. Let's go back to the kitchen." Sharon started across the room to retrieve the adventurous little boy. "Don't you want to help Sharon finish baking the cookies?"

Just before she reached him, he turned. The tow-headed boy's expression was animated with excitement, his blue eyes gleaming. "Horses, horses," he declared and swung around to press his face against the wire-mesh barrier.

With a sinking feeling, Sharon glanced through the screen toward the corral by the barn. A flaxen-maned chestnut horse had nudged the gate open and was taking its first tentative step to freedom. The five other horses in the corral, horses Sharon had contracted to train, were crowding into line behind their chestnut leader.

Her gaze never left the horse warily stepping through the opened gate as she scooped Tony off the floor and swung him onto her hip. She didn't dare leave him alone in the house while she chased the horses back into the corral. Heaven only knew what he'd get into; mischief seemed to be his middle name.

Sharon fumbled with the screen-door latch for a second, then pushed it open to race from the house. The sleek chestnut threw its head up and snorted in alarm at her approach. Her boots skimmed down the porch steps while Tony rode on her hip, laughing with delight.

"Huck! You spoiled, good-for-nothing animal! Get back in there!" she shouted at the troublesome horse, cursing its latest trick of opening the corral gate.

As the chestnut lunged to make good its escape, Sharon ran an intercepting course that would place her directly in the path of the horses and hopefully prevent them from bolting down the ranch lane to the road.

It wasn't easy doing that with Tony on her hip. She didn't dare set him on the ground. With his penchant for adventure, he'd get right into the thick of things, ignorant of any possible danger to himself. In the back of her mind, there was a silent tribute to her mother, who had probably coped with many similar situations raising her two children on this western Colorado ranch.

At her shrill whistles and waving arm, the chestnut horse broke stride. Its hesitation provided Sharon time to get in front of the horses. For a second, she thought the other horses pressing the lead chestnut from the rear might prod it into charging against her.

"Wave your arms and yell real loud, Tony," she enlisted the boy's help in raising a commotion to turn the horses. He thought it was all great fun and threw himself into this new game with such abandon that Sharon nearly dropped him.

The horses swerved, hooves clacking. She had stopped them from galloping down the lane, but herding them back into the corral was another thing. It became a frustrating game of tag. Sharon was able to contain them, but she couldn't coerce the horses to re-enter the fenced enclosure. If only she could get one inside, chances were the others would follow, but each time Sharon tried to lure the horses in, they shied away from the open gate.

Her cowboy boots were not designed for running over rough ground for long periods. Her leg muscles soon began to feel the strain, while Tony was getting heavier and heavier, his weight more awkward to balance. Her arm ached from holding him on her hip, and he didn't help the situation. Weary of the game, Tony wanted it to stop so he could pet the horses. His whining and demanding protests wore on her already frazzled nerves. She was hot and tired, choking on the dust churned up by the milling horses.

Sharon paused a second to catch her breath, wondering how on earth she was going to get the horses back in the corral on her own. Neither her parents nor her brother were due back until evening. She felt doomed.

From out of nowhere it seemed, a brown streak flashed by Sharon. It only took her half a second to recognize Sam, Ridge Halliday's cow dog. She overcame the impulse to turn around and locate its owner. The well-trained dog had already driven the loose horses into a tight circle and was pressing to herd them through the gate. All that was needed to accomplish the feat was her assistance.

With a burst of flagging energy, Sharon pushed

forward. The flashy chestnut made one bold attempt to break from the pack, but the efficient cow dog smoothly turned it back. There was a rippling toss of the horse's flaxen mane, then it whirled and trotted meekly through the corral gate. The other horses followed single file.

While the dog guarded the opening, Sharon rushed to shut the gate. When she set Tony on the ground to secure the gate latch, the muscles in her arm vibrated uncontrollably from the prolonged strain of holding the child. As soon as the gate clicked shut, the panting dog ducked under the lower rail and trotted back to its master, obviously located somewhere behind her.

"Doggie, doggie." Tony lost interest in the horses to begin chasing the smaller, four-footed prey, his clutching hand outstretched in a supplicating gesture.

"Stay here, Tony," Sharon ordered sharply, fully aware the cow dog was not a pet. It required an economy of breath to speak, making her voice tautly low and impatient. "The doggie will bite you."

She spared a glance in Tony's direction long enough to ascertain that he was hesitating, unsure whether or not she was telling him the truth. There was the crunch of an unhurried stride approaching her from behind.

"Did somebody forget to shut the gate?" Ridge Halliday's low, drawling voice ran over her weary body with a soothing laziness.

"No. Wonder Horse in there," Sharon flicked an

irritated look at the gleaming chestnut horse as it began walking docilely toward the gate where the humans were gathered, "opened the gate. Would you bring me a piece of that baling wire by the barn."

She pushed the waving sweep of caramel-colored hair off her perspiring forehead. She was marking time, postponing the moment when she actually had to look at Ridge, and knew it. But she needed the respite to marshal her carefully practiced, light-hearted friendliness.

If there was a course in adolescent crushes getting out of hand, Sharon could have qualified as an expert. Ridge Halliday was a fellow rancher in the basin and a contemporary of her brother—and the embodiment of every woman's fantasy. It wasn't fair to any impressionable teenager to be exposed to a man like him.

As his long shadow fell across hers, Sharon recognized the real problem—she was no longer a teenager, but that didn't stop a quiver of excitement from shooting through her. She took the proffered baling wire from his leather-gloved hand, her glance skimming him while she became irritated because of her hot and disheveled appearance.

An inch over six feet, Ridge had the loose-limbed ease of a rider about him. His long frame was hard and lean, not given to bulging muscles but a sinewed toughness. These same characteristics were stamped on his sun-browned features, except that his hard-bitten looks were made handsome by the lazy glint in his blue eyes and the grooves carved near the corners of his mouth that always seemed to suggest a lurking smile. A dusty brown cowboy hat was pulled low on his forehead, covering most of his mahogany-dark hair except at the back, where its shaggy length curled onto his shirt collar.

All in all, it was a potent combination of hard virility and a lazy sexual charm. There was a surface recklessness about him that seemed to hide the deadly serious side of him. Or so Sharon had always thought. Perhaps it was the case that he took his ranch and his work seriously—and nothing else. There was no doubt in her mind that Ridge could be an outrageous flirt at times. Heaven knew he had flirted with her enough times to lead her into believing she meant something more to him than just his buddy's kid sister, only to learn the painful lesson that with Ridge it was a case of out of sight, out of mind.

While Sharon concentrated on wrapping the baling wire around the gate post and the gate, the blaze-faced chestnut hung its head over the gate and nuzzled her shoulder in an overture of friendship. But she refused to forgive the animal so easily.

"Unless you have wire cutters for teeth, you aren't going to be able to open the gate the next time," she informed the horse as she tightly twined the ends of the wire.

"Beautiful animal," Ridge remarked and stroked the sleek, muscled neck of the horse.

"Beauty is as beauty does," Sharon retorted. "And that horse is close to being worthless. He's the yearling Sue Ann Langford's father spent a fortune for a couple years ago. She's spoiled him to the point where he's nearly ruined. It was a mistake ever to agree to train him for her. Huck is headstrong and unruly, tame as a puppy but completely undisciplined. He's been here only three days and already we've had to padlock the grain bin, nail his stall door shut—and now this."

All her senses were so completely focused on Ridge that for a few moments Sharon had completely forgotten about her young charge until she heard a low growl coming from the mixed-breed dog. The warning growl alternated with an anxious whine as Sharon turned to see Tony crouched over and inching closer to the nervous dog unwilling to leave its master's side to escape the unwanted attention from the child.

In a high, little voice, Tony was trying to coax it to stay still. "Doggie. Nice doggie."

"I told you to leave the dog alone." Sharon moved, scooping Tony again into her aching arms while the dog wiggled with relief now that he was no longer being pursued by this small person. Tony struggled in her arms, wanting to be put down. "The last thing I need today is for you to get bitten," she muttered, because everything had seemed to go from bad to worse. "If it isn't one thing, it's another."

"Why don't you marry me and I'll take you away from all this?" Ridge declared lazily.

She swung around, facing him. He was leaning against the corral, an arm draped carelessly along the top rail, an easy familiarity in his blue eyes that was so unnerving. It didn't seem to matter how many times she heard that joking comment—there was always a little leap of her pulse. But she had also learned not to wear her emotions on her sleeve.

With so much practice, her laugh came naturally. "If I ever said yes to that, you'd run so fast that we'd be seeing your dust for days. You're going to say that to the wrong girl one of these days and find yourself being sued for breach of promise," Sharon warned.

Ridge chuckled, amused rather than annoyed by her response. He pushed away from the fence to move toward her. "Have you got any coffee hot?" In the past, Ridge had frequented the Powell house too often not to feel he could invite himself in for coffee.

"No coffee, but I've got a batch of homemade cookies fresh from the oven," Sharon countered, adopting the role of friend and neighbor that had served her in such good stead the last three years.

"Leave it to a woman to know the way to a man's heart." Slanting her a lazy smile, Ridge hooked a hand companionably on her shoulder. Together they started for the house.

The idle weight of his hand made itself felt, but Sharon had learned how to deal with such things. She had stopped reading anything intimate into his attitude. An arm around her shoulders meant precisely nothing. A kiss here and there meant nothing. She had stopped making mountains out of molehills. She had put aside her childish dreams that someday Ridge would look at her and discover that she was something special. It simply wasn't going to happen. Over the years, she had finally come to accept that and it hadn't been easy.

At first, she had strongly considered leaving home—leaving Colorado and seeking a job training horses somewhere. But something had warned her that Ridge's ghost would follow her and torment her with what-ifs and what-might-have-beens. So she had stayed—to face the situation and come to grips with its harsh reality.

"I want my cookie," Tony complained with a demanding frown.

"Who is the little guy?" Ridge looked around her at the boy riding on her hip again. "I know I haven't seen you the last couple of times I've been over, but not even you can keep a toddler hidden this long."

As he spoke, his gaze ran down her slender curves. He knew very well the child wasn't hers, but it amused him to tease her with the possibility. Once such a remark would have aroused a blush. Now Sharon shrugged it off without a blink of an eye.

"Tony is Rita Campbell's little boy." Rita was an old schoolmate of Sharon's. They were still friends even though marriage, a home and a family, plus a part-time job had severely cut into the free time Rita could devote to that friendship. "Her regular sitter was sick today, so I volunteered to look after Tony," Sharon explained her unusual occupation. "You need to be three people to keep up with him."

In unison, they climbed the porch steps and crossed to the screen door. His hand slipped off her shoulder as he reached in front of her to open the door.

"Stay." It was a low-voiced order issued to the dog trailing after them. With a plaintive whine of protest, the dog obediently sat on its haunches to wait for its master.

Tony twisted around as Ridge closed the door, shutting the dog outside. "Doggie come in and play," he said to Sharon.

"No, the dog has to stay outside," she insisted. "Let's go out to the kitchen and see if somebody ate your cookies while we were gone."

"Doggie wants a cookie." Tony gave her a bright-eyed look that Sharon ignored.

"I take it you're here by yourself today," Ridge inserted.

"Yes. Mom and Dad and Scott are out at the South Meadow gathering the first-calf heifers. It always happens that way, doesn't it?" She smiled in his direction. "Livestock never gets out unless you're the only person around. You could have helped," she said in a half-accusation.

"You and Sam were doing all right," he replied with a faint grin. "I thought I should stay by the lane in case the horses got past the two of you."

"Sure," she mocked him with an exaggerated

agreement. "The truth is you were standing back there so you could watch me racing around there like a mad hen with two-ton Tony on her hip." Upon entering the kitchen, she plunked Tony on his chair and pushed it up to the table. "You'd better finish your cookies and milk," she advised him, but he was still pouting because she wouldn't let the dog come in the house. He hung his head, his lower lip jutting out sullenly, and showed no interest in the cookies or milk.

Ridge wandered over to the kitchen counter where the cookies were cooling on the newspaper. "I'm going to be needing a couple of extra riders at Latigo the day after tomorrow. I stopped by to see if Scott might be able to shake free."

Latigo was the name of his ranch, which encompassed nearly a hundred square miles of Piceance Basin in western Colorado. The rough terrain of hill and gully was well suited for cattle ranching, and Latigo was one of the larger ones in the area.

"I'm sure Scott can help out," Sharon answered. Although her father and brother were ostensibly partners in their ranch, her brother often hired out for day work at neighboring ranches to lessen the drain on the ranch's finances and permit them to put more of the profits back into the ranch.

"Do you suppose I can persuade your mom to come along and cook for us—and maybe swing a rope now and then?" He arched her a querying look as he **bit in**to a cookie.

The corners of her mouth deepened with a faint smile. Her mother was widely respected and sought after as both a cook and a cowhand, although the approval of her skill on horseback was usually grudgingly given. Of course, her father gave full credit to his wife for working at his side and building their ranch from practically nothing to the modest holding it was today. Sharon admired her because even though her mother did a man's work, she never stopped being a woman. She didn't resort to cussing or rough talk to gain male acceptance as one of them. If anything, men respected her more for that.

"You'll have to ask Mom." Sharon didn't answer for her mother.

"What I should do is arrange some sort of package deal for the whole Powell family?" A slow smile widened the line of his mouth.

"That might be arranged." She laughed briefly, pleased by the subtle recognition of her worth as a working rider. After she washed her hands in the sink, she walked to the table to begin spooning the rest of the cookie dough onto the sheet pan. It was easier to keep busy while Ridge was around. It kept her from focusing too much attention on him. "Do you want me to have Scott call you tonight?'

"Yeah, why don't you do that?" he agreed and came over to the table to watch her, a fistful of cookies in his hand. He stood idly for a minute, then pulled out a chair to sit down.

When she carried the pan to the oven, she had to step over his long legs, his boots hooked one atop the other. Ridge always seemed so relaxed, and she always felt so tense. Turning back to the table, she deliberately shifted her attention to the pouting Tony.

"Drink your milk." She pushed the glass closer to him so it was within his reach.

"No. Don't want it," he refused sulkily. "It's warm. I want another glass."

A fresh glass of cold milk from the refrigerator would probably have only one swallow taken from it, then be left to sit as this one had been. In Sharon's opinion, that was a shameful waste.

"You have to drink this milk before you can have any more," she informed him.

"No." Tony slumped in the chair and peered up at her through tearful lashes.

"Don't be so mean," Ridge eyed her with mock reproval. "I don't blame the kid for not wanting warm milk. I don't either."

With an adult supporting his demand, Tony reasserted it, banging his feet against the chair in a slight temper display. "I want milk."

"You're a lot of help," she muttered to Ridge. "I tell him no and you undermine what little authority I have."

There was an amused glint in his eyes at her flash of anger. "There is a simple solution to this that will satisfy both you and Tony," Ridge insisted.

"What's that?" Sharon asked in skeptical challenge.

"Ice." After delivering his one-word answer, he rolled to his feet in a single motion and crossed to the refrigerator, removing a tray of ice cubes from the freezer compartment. "Tony still drinks the same glass of milk, but the ice will make it cold." Taking two cubes from the tray, he walked to the table and dropped them in Tony's glass. "You see?" An eyebrow quirked in Sharon's direction.

"I hope you're right." For some reason, she was still skeptical of his solution.

"Of course I'm right," Ridge said as Tony reached eagerly for the glass.

Instead of drinking the milk, Tony tried to scoop out the ice cubes, and Sharon understood why she had instinctively doubted the wisdom of Ridge's solution.

"No, Tony, don't play with the ice cubes," she admonished and pulled his stubby fingers out of the glass to dry them with a kitchen towel. She slid a dry glance at Ridge. "Terrific idea."

"Drink your milk and see if the ice made it cold." Ridge changed chairs, sitting in the one next to Tony offering him the glass again. "Once you drink all your milk, then you can have the ice cubes." With seeming obedience, Tony took a drink of his milk and Ridge shot a complacent glance at Sharon. "You just have to know how to handle children."

"And you're an expert, of course," she mocked. "How many children did you say you had?"

"None . . . that I know about," he qualified his answer with a roguish twinkle glittering in his eyes.

It wasn't as if half the women in the county wouldn't have been willing to bear his child, Sharon thought. She turned away quickly to the oven to check on the cookies before her gaze lingered on the raw strength and maturity etched in his roughly hewn features. It was much too easy to love him—and much too hard to stop.

The cookies were close enough to being done, so she removed the pan from the oven with the aid of a protective potholder and carried it to the counter. She concentrated on lifting them one by one from the sheet pan with the metal spatula so she could block out the physical impact of his presence.

"Scott mentioned you were planning on cutting back on the number of shows you're attending this year," he remarked.

"I think so," she admitted. "It's getting too expensive to haul horses to some of the distant shows. I thought I'd concentrate on the major shows in the immediate area. I can't quit the show ring altogether or I'll lose the chance of getting new horses to train." She was well aware that competing in stock and western pleasure classes brought her to the attention of owners willing to pay to have their horses trained by a professional. Her reputation as a trainer was growing—and she had a roomful of trophies and ribbons to prove it.

As she turned to carry the empty cookie sheet to the table, she saw Tony slyly dipping his hand into the milk glass. "Tony—"

At her sharply reprimanding tone, he jerked his hand out of the glass. The suddenness of his action tipped the glass over, spilling the milk—right into Ridge's lap.

"Now look what you've done, Tony." But she couldn't keep the smile out of her voice as she deposited the cookie sheet on the table and reached for the towel. Her hazel eyes were dancing with laughter when she met Ridge's glance. "Was the milk cold?" she murmured innocently.

The anger went out of his expression as quickly as it had come in. "You know damned well it was," he muttered with a half smile and took the towel she offered to blot up the excess wetness.

"The ice cubes were your idea." Sharon took delight in reminding him of the fact.

"Maybe father doesn't always know best," Ridge conceded with a rueful look and stood up to wipe at the front of his jeans where the wet blotch spread onto his thigh. "There's one consolation. Milk is probably the cleanest thing that's touched these jeans lately."

The faded material was dusty and dirt-stained, but Sharon was more conscious of the way the work-worn fabric snugly shaped itself to his hips and thighs like a second skin. It turned her thoughts in a direction that had no place in the kitchen.

The spilled milk that hadn't initially landed on Ridge was now dripping off the edge of the table. Sharon grabbed the dishcloth from the sink and mopped up the milky film on the table. All the while Tony stayed very quiet and very small, not wanting to draw further attention to himself in an attempt to avoid possible punishment. He looked sufficiently chagrined so that Sharon didn't feel anything more needed to be said.

As she returned to the sink to rinse the dishcloth under the faucet, Ridge followed her. "I'm afraid your towel is soiled," he said, acknowledging it had picked up some of his dirt along with the milk.

"It'll wash."

# Chapter Two

Taking the towel from him, Sharon draped it over the edge of the counter to dry and folded the dishcloth to lay it over the divider of the double sink. She felt him studying her with a penetrating thoughtfulness and sent him a curious sidelong glance.

"I hear you've been seeing a lot of that oil man lately," Ridge said.

"Oil man?" She frowned with an initial bewilderment, then her expression cleared. "You mean Andy Rivers," she said, realizing suddenly whom he meant. "He's a geologist who *works* for an oil company."

The Piceance Basin of Colorado contained one of the largest concentrations of oil shale. According to Andy, they estimated there were over 500 billion barrels of recoverable oil in the shale, more than the provable reserves of crude oil in the OPEC countries. It defied imagination when one considered they were standing on top of it.

"Same difference," Ridge shrugged at her answer and continued to study her with a kind of interested speculation. "Is it true it's become a regular thing?"

"More or less. Between his work schedule and my horse show dates, we don't see each other all that frequently," Sharon insisted. "But I suppose we go out on a fairly regular basis."

"Are you thinking about marrying him?" he asked.

Just for a second she searched his face, trying to find some reason for this personal interest, but there appeared to be little more than the casual interest of a family friend. She suppressed a sigh. Friends always seemed to be more inquisitive than family.

She laughed shortly and with little humor. "Why is it that if a girl sees a guy more than a half-dozen times everybody assumes she's planning on a trip to the alter? Maybe I'm just taking a page out of your book—or Scott's." She was vaguely impatient, but there was no heat of anger in her voice.

His eyes narrowed speculatively. "What do you mean by that?"

"You and Scott seem to be on the road to becoming confirmed bachelors." To her knowledge, neither Ridge nor her brother had been serious about any girl they had dated. "Maybe I'm not the marrying kind either." Her real problem was that she had to stop comparing every man she met to Ridge. Until she did that, she probably never would find a man she could care enough about to marry. "I enjoy going out with Andy. We have fun together."

Which was true. Andy made her laugh. When she was with him, she rarely thought about Ridge. Maybe that didn't seem earth shattering, but she considered it important.

"The three of us used to have some good times together. You, me and Scott," Ridge stated somewhat absently. Lifting a hand, he trailed a finger along her cheekbone and tucked a strand of hair behind her ear. "Didn't we?"

"Yes." Sharon didn't trust herself to say more.

There was a poignant drift of memories back to that time he had recalled. It had always been a threesome, although Sharon had been so wildly infatuated with Ridge at the time that she had believed her brother was tagging along with them—instead of her tagging along with them. She had built so many dreams from those innocent evenings in Ridge's company. She had wanted so much to believe he loved her that she had exaggerated every slow dance, every kiss, out of all proportion.

Long ago Sharon had stopped trying to second-guess his motives, so she didn't allow herself to wonder whether he was caught in a past memory when his calloused fingers laid themselves against the curve of her neck. He bent his head toward her, the brim of his hat partially masking the skimming inspection of his gaze.

She had learned that a kiss from Ridge was nothing more than a kiss. Avoiding it would make more out of it than what it was. The trick was to accept it *without* making more out of it than it was.

The warm pressure of his mouth covered her lips and moved familiarly to take possession. His hand tightened slightly on her neck to arch her into the kiss. An encircling arm was bringing her against his body. Sharon relaxed naturally against his hard frame, letting her hands slide around his middle.

Her lips moved under the investigative influence of his. The stirrings of hunger escaped her restraint and became a part of her response. Sharon wavered, wanting to draw back from the edge of this unexpected precipice, but Ridge pressed the issue with deepening insistence. Her indecision dissolved under the heat of raw longing.

There was a slow disentangling of their lips. Her breath was coming low and shallow, as disturbed as the uneven rhythm of her pulse. Sharon was careful not to let her expression show just how much his kiss had affected her. Her gaze she kept focused on the shoulder seam of his shirt. His face remained close to hers, his hat brim casting a shadow on her face while his moist breath warmed her hot skin.

"When did you learn to kiss like that?' His low voice held a hint of curious amusement.

The hand on the small of her back spread its fingers, testing the supple curve of her spine. It sent little waves of heat lightning flashing through her nerves, recharging their high sensitivity. His hard, sinewed length seemed indelibly imprinted on her flesh, male in its contours.

"It's been two years or more since you kissed me." If he'd asked, Sharon could have told him the place and the time. Her voice contained no trace of her tension, even though it was a little on the husky side. "I've had time to practice. Surely you didn't expect me to kiss like some innocent seventeen-year-old."

"I don't know," Ridge murmured and raised her chin, his blue eyes intent and probing in their narrowed study of her. "But I didn't expect this."

This recognition of her as a woman was the very thing she had so longed to hear. Her breath caught in her throat, as she hardly dared to believe it. Even if Ridge meant nothing beyond that, there was sweet satisfaction in being acknowledged as a desirable female. However, both her feet remained firmly planted in reality. It was the first time Sharon had met him on an equal footing—man to woman. He didn't have a starry-eyed romantic in his arms.

All this gave her a new confidence when his mouth sought to discover the mystery of her lips again. It wasn't necessary to disguise her enjoyment of this intimacy. Her lips parted under the deepening urgency of his kiss. A golden tide of warmth curled through her limbs while she spread her hands over the rippling muscles of his back.

Her senses were awash with the taste, the feel, and the smell of him. His mouth rolled off her lips as he came up for air, the heat of his breath fanning her cheek. There was a labored edge to his breathing, and her acutely sensitive hearing picked up the slightly uneven tempo of his heartbeat.

There was a bright glint in his eyes when Sharon finally lifted her gaze to meet his. Behind its surface amusement, the look was faintly accusing.

"You've come of age," Ridge murmured.

"I turned twenty-one on my last birthday," she pointed out, a fact that he had obviously over-looked, being so accustomed to regarding her as Scott's kid sister.

From the front porch there came a snarling growl that erupted into an angry bark. Sharon stiffened at the sound, then pushed out of Ridge's arms.

"Tony," she gasped the toddler's name as she raced into the living room. He had managed to push the screen door open. When he heard her coming, he hurriedly tossed the cookie at the barking dog and guiltily let the door swing shut.

"Doggie wanted a cookie." He blinked at her with wide-eyed innocence.

Fully aware that Tony was trying to make her believe he had intended throwing the treat to the dog all the time, Sharon wasn't buying any of it. The cookie had been offered in an attempt to entice the dog inside the house.

"All right, bud. It's nap time for you," Sharon informed him angrily.

The minute she picked him up Tony started wailing at the top of his lungs. "Don't want nap!" he protested. His cries immediately started the dog barking.

Between the two, Sharon was nearly deafened. She shouted at both of them to hush up, but neither listened. When she turned, she spied Ridge leaning an arm against the doorway to the kitchen and watching the scene with detached amusement.

"Will you shut that dog up!" she demanded.

"Sam. Quiet." The two words came out hard and quick. There was instant silence from the dog, although Tony continued his whining bawl in her ear. Ridge's smile was close to a taunting grin as he moved lazily toward the door on a path that took him past Sharon. "One way or another, I think Sam and I have done enough damage for one afternoon." His glance flicked to her lips and she guessed they were still swollen from his kisses. "Don't forget to have Scott phone me tonight."

"I won't." But she'd practically forgotten the reason Ridge had stopped in the first place until he reminded her. Being in his arms had driven nearly everything from her mind.

The instant Tony realized the dog was leaving too, he sent out a fresh protest. Ridge and Sam were long gone before Sharon was finally able to quiet him down. Although he tried very hard to stay awake, Tony was exhausted from all the excitement and eventually fell asleep against his will.

When the ranch house was at last filled with silence, Sharon returned to the kitchen to put the last sheet of cookies into the oven. It was impossible not to think about Ridge. The scent of him still clung to her clothes and her skin, and the remembered sensation of his roaming hands remained with her.

She was determined not to make a mountain out of this molehill-sized kiss the way she'd done in the past. To paraphrase an old saying—one kiss did not a romance make. But it gave her a lot to think about.

Ridge—so easygoing and carefree on the surface. But there was more to the man than that, even if he never showed the serious side of himself around her. It existed—of that she had no doubt. No one could approach life with the shallow and lackadaisical indifference that Ridge showed and efficiently manage a ranch the size of Latigo. If that was the true sort of man he was, the ranch would have started going downhill five years earlier, when Ridge took over after his father's death. That hadn't happened. From the talk Sharon had heard, the Latigo was in a more solid financial position than it had enjoyed in years.

Her brother Scott probably knew Ridge better than anyone, but getting him to talk was about as difficult as extracting oil from shale economically. Scott was undoubtedly a bonanza of information, but Sharon hadn't successfully squeezed any of it from him.

When the last of the cookies were cooling on the counter, she began washing up the baking dishes. It was funny to discover that as a teenager she had been attracted to the slightly wild and fun-loving side of Ridge, always ripe for a laugh and a good time. Now that she had grown older—and hopefully wiser—she was becoming more intrigued by the more silent, and probably stronger, side of him.

It was nearly six in the evening when Rita came by the house to pick up Tony. She had to rush home to fix supper, so there wasn't time for Sharon to have more than a quick chat with her while they gathered all Tony's toys and clothing.

Supper was in the oven and Sharon had the evening chores done when the pickup truck with the horse trailer crested a hillock and approached the barns. Sharon waved to the three people crowded together in the cab of the truck and continued to the house. With their horses to be unsaddled, rubbed down, and fed for the night, it would be another quarter of an hour before they joined her, Sharon knew.

By the time Sharon's parents and brother had taken turns using the shower, three-quarters of an hour had passed before they all sat down at the table. There was a moment's pause while her father said grace. Lloyd Powell was tall and broadly muscled, with a silver mane of hair that had once been the color of his thirty-two-year-old son's dusty brown hair. Scott had his wide features, bluntly chiseled and weathered brown by the sun and wind, but he had his mother's green eyes. On the other hand, Sharon had inherited her mother's slender build and toffee-colored hair, and her father's hazel-brown eyes.

"I noticed the corral gate is wired shut," her father remarked. "Trouble again?"

"I think I'm going to change Huck's name to Trouble." Sharon identified the chestnut as the culprit and explained about the afternoon's fiasco—and Ridge's timely arrival, passing on Ridge's request for Scott to phone him that evening about working a couple of days for the Latigo.

"Day after tomorrow?" Scott repeated and glanced questioningly at his father. "I should be able to manage that with no problem."

"None that I can see," Lloyd Powell agreed with a slow nod.

"How did the baby-sitting go today?" her mother inquired.

"Don't ask," Sharon replied with a rueful grimace. "I'm convinced no woman in her right mind would take on the task of motherhood if she knew in advance what it was like. You need three sets of arms, feet, and eyes to keep up with them."

"Now you know what it was like having you two," her mother laughed, her sparkling green glance darting between her son and daughter.

"Is that why you waited until I was older before you had Sharon?" Scott wanted to know, drawing attention to their twelve-year age difference. "So you could have a built-in baby-sitter?"

"Your son was a bit slow figuring that one out," his mother declared as she cast a side glance at her husband.

"*My* son? When did he cease being ours and become mine?" he challenged good-naturedly.

Sharon eyed her brother with a studying look.

"Isn't it time you were thinking about getting married and raising a family?" she asked. "By rights, there should already be another generation of Powells running around the house."

"Me?" He was startled and amused by her suggestion. "First, there's a little matter of a bride. If you're so eager for the folks to have grandchildren, why don't you marry your oil man?"

She lifted her head. "So you're the one who told Ridge about Andy."

Her brother appeared slightly taken aback and a little uncomfortable. "Was your boyfriend supposed to be a secret?"

"No." She smiled at the thought. "At the moment, that's all Andy happens to be—a friend. It's just that Ridge referred to him as an oil man when he asked me about him this afternoon. I wasn't aware my love life was something you two discussed."

"We don't," Scott replied evenly.

"What do you talk about?" Her curiosity was heightened by an afternoon spent wondering about such things and what they might reveal about Ridge.

"What kind of a question is that?" Scott frowned at her as if she'd asked a ridiculous question. "What does anybody talk about? Me? You? Dad?"

Put in that context, it did sound a little silly. She poked a fork at her food and shrugged. "I just wondered what men talk about."

"The weather, business, their health—and

women," her father answered, "but not necessarily in that order. If they're married, you can add family to the list. Not a very mysterious list, is it?"

"No." Sharon had to laugh at her attempt to make something complicated out of a simple statement.

As soon as the meal was finished, Scott left the table to ring through to the Latigo ranch. Sharon helped her mother clear the table, stowing the leftovers in the refrigerator and stacking the dishes in the sink to wash.

"Mom!" Scott called to her from the front room. "Ridge wondered if you would be able to cook for the crew. And he wants to know if Sharon can lend a hand too."

"Tell him," her father inserted before either could answer, "that I don't know if I like the idea of him hiring away my whole crew." It was meant as a good-natured gibe between friends.

There was a moment's pause while Scott relayed the message, then came back with a reply. "Ridge says that's the risk you take when you have a good crew willing to work cheap. It isn't his fault we work for you for nothing."

Sharon heard her father's hearty chuckle and walked to the doorway. "Scott, tell Ridge I can spare two days." The new horses she was working would probably benefit from a short respite from the training routine. "But—I don't come cheap. If he wants me, he'll have to pay top dollar."

Scott repeated her answer into the telephone. A

grin split his face at the response. "I don't think I'll tell her the last part."

"Tell me what?" she insisted with a wary look.

He placed a covering hand over the mouthpiece. "Ridge said he doesn't mind paying you top dollar." He hesitated, the light in his eyes dancing brighter.

"Is that all?" Sharon knew it wasn't.

"Not quite." Scott tried to contain his smile. "He said there's always more than one way to get your money's worth out of a woman."

"Tell him not to worry. I come with a money-back guarantee if not completely satisfied." This time she was the one with the gleam in her eye and Scott was the one hesitant about passing on the message.

Her father cleared his throat and reached for his cigar. Her mother had appeared in the doorway behind Sharon and he arched her a considering look. "Might be that you should go along with this young girl of yours, Lena."

"*My* girl?" she countered. "She sounds more like you." But she glanced at her son. "Tell him I'll stop over tomorrow and check the camp kitchen and supplies to make sure nothing's been forgotten." She didn't wait to hear Scott relaying her message as she nudged Sharon's arm. "Do you want to wash or dry the dishes?"

"I'll wash." She turned and followed her mother to the kitchen sink.

When she turned on the faucets, the noise of

running water drowned out the sound of her brother's telephone conversation in the front room. Mechanically Sharon began washing the glasses first, but her thoughts were turned ahead. She had never worked with Ridge before, so she couldn't help wondering about this new kind of experience with him. But she was careful not to start imagining possibilities.

"I thought you liked Andy," her mother remarked, interrupting her silent reverie.

"I do." Sharon glanced at her in surprise.

"At the table tonight, you seemed to stress the point that he is just a friend." She took a great deal of time to wipe one glass when she usually zipped over it with a few efficient swipes of the towel.

"He is a friend," Sharon insisted. "If I was trying to make anything clear, it was simply that I'm not on the verge of marrying him—as everybody seems to think."

"You mean Scott?"

"And Ridge, too."

The mention of his name by Sharon produced a long, heavy silence. Her mother was completely aware of Sharon's previous infatuation with Ridge, and how Sharon had loved him with the blind intensity only an adolescent can attain. She didn't wish to raise the subject with Sharon because she knew what a long and painful process it had been getting over that unrequited crush.

"After he left this afternoon, Mom," Sharon spoke softly into the silence, "I had the strange feeling that I don't know him at all. I built up such a dream around him that I never saw him—just my dream."

"That's usually the way it is," her mother nodded.

"Around me, Ridge is always laughing and joking—or that's the way he's seemed." She frowned and dipped another glass into the sudsy water.

"Perhaps that's the only level of communication he's had with you," her mother suggested.

"What do you mean?" Sharon's frown deepened as she turned her curious gaze toward her mother.

" 'When I was a child, I spake as a child,' " she murmured the Biblical quote, becoming vaguely thoughtful. "You were young and carefree, always so quick to laugh and have fun. Whenever the conversation became serious at the table, you used to complain it was boring."

"Well, I'm a woman now," Sharon said with the full-blown confidence she'd found this afternoon, "and I've put away my childish things." She paused to look thoughtfully out the window. The evening darkness on the other side gave the glass a mirror-like quality, reflecting an indistinct image of herself. "It's going to be interesting to meet Ridge as an adult."

"Sharon . . . you're not—"

The hesitancy and veiled warning in her mother's voice made her smile. "No, Mom, I'm not still crazy about him. That's one of the childish things I've put behind me."

The events of that afternoon had put her on a

new footing with Ridge, but Sharon didn't intend to replace puppy love with passion. Both were equally blinding emotions. And she didn't plan to walk down another dead-end street.

Spring had exploded on the rugged plateau, turning the seemingly barren terrain into a patchwork of color. Sharon walked the close-coupled bay horse, a Latigo brand burned on its hip, through a grove of aspen trees growing on the north slope below the ridgeline. She was making one last sweep through this section of range for any strays that might have escaped the first roundup before joining the crew at the holding pens.

Bushes of chokecherry and serviceberry crowded close under the shade of the aspens. The leaves overhead formed a glittering, silvery-green canopy that trembled at the slightest stirring of air. Showy blooms of blue columbine, the Colorado state flower, blanketed the ground in the aspen grove.

Emerging from the stand of aspens, Sharon kept her horse pointed down the slope toward the sage-covered valley. The muted purple-green color of the sage was interspersed with patches of wildflowers, the brilliant crimsons and scarlets of Indian paintbrush, firecracker penstemon, and scarlet gilia.

The air was sharp and clear, the morning sun pressing its warmth on her the instant she left the coolness of the north slope. Sharon reined in the bay horse and peeled off her jacket, tying it behind her saddle. Her flannel shirt of green and gold plaid was adequate covering on this exceptionally mild spring day.

A ribbon of green wound crookedly through the valley of sage, marking the course of a small creek. The scattering of cottonwood and willow trees growing along the banks offered potential conceal-ment for an odd cow or two. Taking up the reins again, Sharon urged the bay horse into a canter and headed for the creek to investigate.

The small creek was full from the winter runoff, and the water ran swiftly over its shallow bed in a rushing murmur. There were no cattle in sight, nothing larger than a mule deer disturbed into flight by Sharon's approach. Still, she continued to walk her horse along the wide band of tall grass beside the creek. The scene was too idyllic to leave, and the general direction of the stream was one she would have taken anyway.

The strides of her horse made quick, swishing sounds in the thick rye grass that nearly reached her stirrup. Once this grass had dominated the landscape the way the sage did now, until early cattlemen had allowed their cattle to overgraze it. The Ute Indians had given this country its name, *Piceance,* which means "tall grass." Now the grass, properly called Big Basin wild rye, grew only along isolated stream beds flowing into Piceance Creek.

The bay horse whickered softly and tugged at the bit, pricking its ears toward the silver rush of water. Her own mouth felt dry after the long morning ride, so Sharon reined the horse toward a gravel bar that pushed into the stream a few yards ahead.

When they reached the narrow bar, Sharon dismounted and let the horse bury its muzzle in the cool, clear water and suck in the liquid in noisy slurps. She removed her hat and shook her shoulder-length hair free after hours of being tucked under the crown. After the horse had satisfied its thirst, she moved a short way upstream and stretched flat on the gravel to scoop up several handfuls of water, laying her hat on the ground beside her. For safety's sake, she kept hold of the reins. The bay horse appeared to be well trained but she wasn't taking any chances.

# Chapter Three

The water was crystal clear and cold, revealing the smooth and glistening stones on the creek bottom. Sharon had taken her last drink when she felt a pull on the reins. She tightened her grip on them quickly and hastily looked up. The solid-colored bay had lifted its head in sudden alertness to stare at some distant object across the creek. It snorted loudly, then its sides heaved in a questioning whicker.

As she pushed to her feet, wiping her wet hand on her jeans, she heard the drumming of a horse's hooves growing steadily louder. She shielded her eyes with her hand to look into the sun and identify the approaching rider.

The tall, lean shape could belong to no one but Ridge Halliday. A thread of uncertainty ran through her nerves at the prospect of meeting him here. Sharon was puzzled by the cause of it. She hadn't seen him since the dawn hours when he'd assigned the crew their individual tasks. There had been no resemblance to the joking, smiling Ridge

Halliday she knew. Perhaps she'd been put off by the hard, authoritative figure he had presented. It had been all business and no nonsense. And Sharon hadn't been sure how to react to this change even though she had come expressly to discover it.

Her hat was on the ground near her feet. Sharon turned and bent to pick it up as Ridge slowed the liver-colored chestnut gelding into a long-striding walk. She heard his horse splashing across the creek to the gravel bar where she was standing and made a project of adjusting her hat snugly on her head before blandly turning to greet him.

The saddle leather creaked as Ridge stepped down, the gravel crunching beneath his boot. His hard features had relaxed out of the stern lines of the morning. There was a faint curve to his mouth, and the rich blue of his eyes was lit by a taunting gleam. Sharon felt a vague relief that this was the Ridge she knew.

"Looks like I caught you loafing on the job," he remarked as his horse dipped its nose into the clear-running creek.

"Just watering my horse the same as you're doing," she retorted, matching his faintly complacent smile with one of her own.

"I had the distinct impression you were lying down when I rode up," Ridge countered and let the reins fall to trail the ground.

"I was getting a drink. The water's icy cold and fresh," Sharon stated, all her senses coming alert as he leisurely approached her.

"So you were taking a break." His skimming glance was playing havoc with her pulse. That purely physical attraction was asserting its influence over her again. "That's going to cost you."

It was crazy. Sparks of sexual disturbance were shooting all over the place, charging the air with an elemental tension that Sharon wanted to avoid.

"That's where you're wrong, Ridge." She calmly applied the brakes to the situation before it could flare into something more than a stimulating exchange of banter.

"What's this?" He halted, smiling through his faintly puzzled frown. "I thought I had a money-back guarantee if I wasn't satisfied."

"Money-back guarantee," Sharon repeated the phrase to stress it. "And that's all you get."

She looped the reins over the bay's head and moved to the left side to mount. His hand closed on her arm, checking her step into the stirrup. She partially turned her head to give him a sidelong look, her glance forced to angle upwards because of his height. His piercing look was hard and probing, and the line of his mouth had a grimness to it.

"What's going on?" he demanded. "Why the cold shoulder all of a sudden?"

The warmth of his hand filtered through her shirt sleeve and spread through her arm. She supposed he was entitled to some explanation for her change in attitude, although she was reluctant to make one. The muscles in her throat were tightening.

"I'm not upset or angry," Sharon insisted. "I just didn't feel like going through with your little charade."

The pressure of his hand increased to turn her away from the saddle and toward him, subjecting her to the scrutiny of his unrelenting gaze. "Why? Because I was making an excuse to kiss you?" Ridge challenged, bringing his intention out in the open even though both of them knew it was where the conversation had been leading all along. "Or didn't you want to be kissed?"

"Not particularly." She lowered her gaze to the width of his leanly muscled shoulders, conscious of the way his chest expanded under his shirt. His nearness was creating an inner agitation she couldn't control.

"You raised no objections the other afternoon," he reminded her tersely. "In fact, you were more than willing."

"Maybe I'm just tired of playing games," she retorted with an impatient edge to her voice.

His harsh laugh had no humor in it. "What do you call this if it isn't playing hard-to-get?"

The accusation startled her into meeting his narrowed look. After those early years of chasing him, was this a subconscious attempt to have Ridge pursue her?

"No." It was more an answer to her own silent question than a denial of his charge.

She started to shrug out of his grip and turn back to the saddle, but Ridge tightened his hold and hooked an arm around her waist to keep her facing him. Anger flared at his forceful tactics. She brought her hands up to keep from being drawn into his arms.

A stillness claimed him. Sharon wasn't about to antagonize him by struggling further, satisfied to show a resistance and keep the status quo. She could feel the coiled energy in his rigidly flexed muscles, the strength held severely in check. Hard blue eyes relentlessly probed her expression.

Suddenly the clenched line of his jaw relaxed. "I get it," he murmured with chilling satisfaction. "You planned all this just to pay me back."

"Wh . . . what?" Sharon faltered, completely thrown by his conclusion because she had no idea what he meant.

"You wanted me to become interested in you so you could have the chance to tell me to go to hell." His mouth crooked in a slanting line of rueful amusement. "I never would have suspected you of being vindictive, Sharon."

"I'm not," she denied his assessment.

"Am I supposed to believe that you're not trying to pay me back for the way I unwittingly hurt you a few years ago?" Ridge tipped his head to the side, hard amusement gleaming in his eyes.

"Then you know—" She stopped in midsentence, briefly horrified to discover he had known how crazy she had been about him.

"When a young girl starts mooning over you like a lovesick puppy, it's difficult to ignore." His voice was thick with silent laughter, the corners of his mouth deepening.

Sharon pulled all her feelings tightly inside her-self to hide them. "It must have been very amusing for you," she replied stiffly. "No wonder you and Scott were so willing to take me with you all the time. I was always good for a laugh if things got dull."

"Sharon." He gave her a little shake as if exas-perated with the deprecating way she was talking about herself. "It wasn't until the last that I guessed the way you felt about me."

"And before that?" Sharon looked at him, so cool that she felt frozen inside. "Why did you drag me along?"

There was a flash of impatience. "Why are you asking me questions when you know the answers are going to hurt?"

"I always thought it was the truth that hurt," she declared, a bitter tinge in her response. "Or maybe I'm just a glutton for punishment. But I would like to know."

Ridge studied her as if to assure himself that she meant it, then grimly set about answering her. "I guess we regarded you as a kind of mascot—a cute and cuddly little mascot."

"Cuddly." Sharon choked on the word. Sudden-ly she was tired of blaming herself for what had happened. "You didn't exactly treat me like a mascot, Ridge," she accused. "You did hand out some encouragement."

"Inadvertently I suppose I did," he admitted, then hit back without pulling any punches. "But you made it plain that you wanted to be kissed.

You did everything but come right out and ask. The first few times I thought you were trying some innocent experimenting on me. Later on I realized that wasn't the case." He paused, a nerve twitching along his jaw. "Hero worship can be very flattering to a man, Sharon, even when it is misplaced," Ridge added curtly.

"I'm sure it can be." It all seemed very fresh and painful. She was beginning to feel the strain of keeping all emotion inside.

"It was never my intention to hurt you—and it isn't now." He sounded slightly angry that she had resurrected the past.

"I don't know." There was something stilted in her voice and the attempted shrug of her shoulders. "I always heard catharsis is good for the soul."

"Wrong. Confession is good for the soul," Ridge corrected her wording. "My God, how did we get into this discussion?" In a burst of impatience, he released her and took a quick stride away.

"You brought it up," Sharon reminded him.

"I'm sorry—" He swung around with thinly disguised impatience. "Sorry I mentioned it—and I'm sorry if you got hurt. What else can I say?"

"Nothing," she agreed, but the apology seemed flat.

His features appeared to grow hard, the recklessly handsome lines smoothed out of them. "I suppose you're secretly wishing that I'd say something like 'I've been waiting all this time for you to grow up'—that I've always been in love with you."

Anger flashed in her hazel eyes at his mildly sarcastic taunt. "Maybe once I might have wanted to hear that, but I don't now."

"It's a damned good thing, because it isn't true," he muttered thickly. "I didn't like it on that damned pedestal. I'm a man, not some god to be adored."

"Believe me, I don't have you on a pedestal any more." Her voice trembled on an angry pitch, a direct reaction to his icy rage.

"Good. At least we're clear on that point." There was a certain rawness in the contained energy that directed his movements as Ridge gathered up the reins to his horse and swung into the saddle.

In direct contrast, Sharon mounted with a deliberate lack of haste. When both toes were securely tucked into the stirrups, she looked at him expectantly, meeting his boldly challenging gaze.

"One more thing before we ride to the holding pens," he said.

"What's that?" Coolly she continued to hold his gaze.

"The next time I decide to kiss you, I won't make any excuses or wait for any invitations. I'll simply do it—man to woman," Ridge stated flatly—and about as unromantically as one could get.

"Always supposing I let you," she countered smoothly, finding she had no qualms about slapping him down—figuratively. There was even the faintest smile on her face when she said it.

"I think I liked you better when you were all honey and sweetness," he muttered.

"And I liked you better when you were just a handsome flirt," she retaliated in kind.

Digging her heels into the bay's sides, she sent the horse across the creek at a lunging canter. Its scrambling hooves kicked back sprays of water, showering the liver-colored chestnut and its rider. She hadn't ridden twenty yards before Ridge caught up with her. Not a word was exchanged during the ride to the holding pens. A couple of times, Sharon stole a glance at his profile, its lines showing such unyielding hardness and his gaze always directed to the front.

The holding pens were a hive of activity. Dust kicked up by churning hooves hung over the scene like a dirty gray pall. The bawling of cattle, clacking hooves, and shouts from cowboys both afoot and on horseback created a ceaseless cacophony. As Sharon and Ridge approached the pens, they separated. Sharon rode over to the motorized cook wagon where her mother was in full preparation for the noon meal, and Ridge headed for the chutes to check on the morning's progress.

Feeding nearly two dozen hungry men with hearty appetites was no easy task under normal circumstances, so Sharon opted to pitch in and help her mother rather than join the crew at the chutes, vaccinating and ear-tagging calves. Conversation was held to a minimum by the amount of work to be done and the noisy competition from the pens.

When the call for noon break sounded, the activity shifted to the camp kitchen. Good-natured grumbling was customary, but this group grumbled with silent expressions. Her brother was one of the last in line. Sharon speared a charred steak and forked it onto his plate.

"What's the matter?" she murmured, her glance running curiously around the vaguely sullen group. "Nobody seems to be in a very good mood."

"It's Ridge," Scott muttered in a grudging fashion. "He's been as bad tempered as a range bull with a nose full of quills. He'd better start letting up or he's going to find himself without a crew."

Scott drew in a deep breath, briefly meeting her sobered glance, and moved on down the line for his helping of potatoes and corn. She scanned the scattered collection of cowboys sitting cross-legged on the ground or clustered around the odd barrel drum. But there was no sign of Ridge among them.

"That should be the last of them," her mother said as she wiped her brow with the back of her hand, a sight in her flop-brimmed hat, a cast-off flannel shirt of her husband's rolled up at the sleeves, and snug-fitting jeans that showed her still very trim figure.

Sharon glanced at the cowboy walking away with a plate mounded with food. "Where's Ridge?" she asked. "I don't remember seeing him come through the line."

"That's right. He didn't," her mother commented with a curious frown and looked around as Sharon had done earlier. "He can help himself when he comes. Grab yourself a plate. If Ridge is like your father, he won't show up until the food is cold. I used to wonder if your father ever ate a hot meal when he was running a crew. That's half the reason I started cooking," she admitted, smiling faintly.

When another quick search of the area couldn't find Ridge, Sharon reached for a plate. It had been a long time since breakfast. Maybe some of her rawness was caused by hunger.

The excuse her mother had offered for Ridge's absence was a reasonable one. From her own experience, Sharon knew her father always lagged behind, making sure everything was in readiness for the crew when they went back to work and no time would be lost. He was always the last one to eat and the first one to throw in his plate. There was no reason to think Ridge was any different.

Her plate was filled and balanced on her knees as she sat on the running board of the van. She was chewing her first bite of steak when Ridge approached the edge of the circle. The camp kitchen was situated upwind from the pens, so the dust and smell would blow away from the food and the noise would also be carried away from them. He was leading a roan horse, instead of the liver-colored chestnut he'd been riding in the morning.

"Hobbs, where did you pick up that unbranded yearling bull?" Ridge snapped the question at his lanky foreman. "How come you haven't separated him into a pen away from those cows?"

"Damned thing's half-wild. We spent nearly an

hour this morning trying to pen it, then finally decided it was easier to separate the cows from him," the foreman Hobbs answered and immediately forked another mouthful of food.

"Is the yearling one of ours?"

Hobbs had to chew quickly to answer. "Yup. It sticks close to that half-shorthorn cow. I reckon she's his momma. I think we had her listed last year as being barren. I figure she hid that calf from us all this time."

"Did you try penning her first?" There was a faintly sarcastic edge to Ridge's voice. Sharon could almost see the foreman's hackles rise at the insulting tone.

"Nope. We didn't do that," he admitted.

There was no comment from Ridge, but his look said it all. "I'll pen her up myself." He stepped into the stirrup and swung onto the saddle all in one motion.

"If you wait a couple of minutes, I'll give you a hand," Hobbs protested.

"I don't need it." Ridge set the roan horse on its haunches and pivoted it in a half-spin, pointing it toward the corrals.

There were a few low mutters, but no one moved from their positions. Sharon was conscious that all were watching as Ridge rode his horse into the largest of the pens. After he had herded the mixed cattle to the far end, he came back and opened the gate to a small pen. He walked the roan horse back to the herd, picked out his quarry, and set about cutting it from the rest.

A sudden movement caught her attention. She turned, spying her brother as he set his half-finished meal down and walked over to the horses, climbing aboard his afternoon mount. Secretly she was relieved that someone had gone to help Ridge, although she suspected he could have managed alone.

With Scott on hand to turn back the cattle, Ridge made short work of separating the shorthorn cow and maneuvering her into the smaller pen. The yearling bull turned out to be a real test for horse and rider. Four times he escaped and rejoined the herd. The fifth time, Ridge threw a loop around his stubby horns and dragged him the length of the pen, shouting to Scott to open the gate.

The sight of the lowing cow in the pen checked the struggles of the yearling bull. Ridge shook off the loop as the yearling trotted eagerly past him through the open gate. A murmur of approval began to flow through the watching riders at the efficient job Ridge had made of it.

A moment later everything went wrong. The instant the yearling heard the squeak of the closing gate Scott had started to swing shut, it whirled and charged for that narrow gap of freedom. The cow followed her feral son.

In a lightning move, Ridge was out of the saddle and lending his strength to Scott's in an effort to latch the gate before the pair forced it open. For a second, it looked as if they were going to succeed. Sharon was on her feet, unconsciously holding her breath.

The gate popped open. Scott was thrown to the side, but Ridge stumbled into the path of the yearling bull and the cow. He tried to dodge out of the way, but the wild-eyed bull hooked at him and drove him onto the ground with a butt of his head. Then both animals were trampling over him and running to rejoin the herd.

For a paralyzed instant, Sharon stood there, staring at Ridge and waiting for him to move out of the half-crumpled ball he'd made of himself on the ground. The sounds of others running toward the scene finally galvanized her into action.

Later, she couldn't even remember climbing the fence and racing across the churned-up sod of the pen. She didn't remember seeing any of the other riders—only her brother as he knelt over Ridge's still form.

And her mother's voice, saying, "Don't move him."

Then Sharon was kneeling on the ground next to him. Her hand felt cold as ice when she pressed it to the side of Ridge's warm neck, seeking his pulse. Her own heart was pounding so loudly that she couldn't hear his, but Sharon felt the vein throbbing beneath her fingers.

Ridge stirred, moaning. There was an ashen pallor to his skin beneath its burnt-in tan. He made an attempt to uncurl from his protective ball and roll onto his back. Her eyes widened at the sight of his torn shirt, the front nearly shredded by sharp, cloven hooves. His stomach was scraped raw, but there were no other obvious wounds.

Suddenly his glazed blue eyes looked directly into Sharon's. "Help me up." His voice was a hoarse, rasping sound, completely unrecognizable as belonging to him.

Somebody ventured the opinion, "Maybe he's just got the wind knocked out of him."

"Probably broke some ribs," someone else said.

"You'd better lie still," Sharon told him and glanced at her mother.

"No." The protest was a guttural sound.

After a few seconds' hesitation, her mother suggested, "Let's see if we can't roll him onto his back."

"Help me up." This time Ridge didn't waste his throat-rough appeal on either Sharon or her mother, directing it instead at Scott who would understand the manly need to rise above injury.

Her mother placed a restraining hand on her son's arm when he would have helped Ridge. She bent closer so that Ridge could see her face. "The pain. Where is the pain, Ridge?' She spoke slowly and concisely.

The tightly clenched jaw, the betraying whiteness, and the trembling mouth that wouldn't let any sound come out were all indications that he was in a great deal of pain. Both arms were clasped around his middle, holding his stomach.

It seemed a very long time before Ridge attempted to answer the question. "My gut—" his voice was so tight and hoarse that tears pricked Sharon's eyes "—feels like it's . . . on fire."

Mrs. Powell sent a concerned glance at her son.

57

"I think he's hurt internally. Get one of the trucks in here and find some blankets."

Somebody handed Sharon a canteen. She vaguely recalled hearing that a person bleeding internally shouldn't drink. So she took her kerchief from her pocket and wetted it down, then used it to moisten Ridge's lips and wipe some of the grime off his face. His features were twisted with pain that had him doubled up.

When the pickup roared into the pen, two cowboys hopped out of the rear bed before it came to a stop. Both carried blankets. Her mother instructed them to roll Ridge onto the blankets and use them as a stretcher to transport him to the back of the truck.

"Dammit! If somebody would just help me . . . , I can walk," he protested in a hoarse rage.

"Hell, what difference will it make now?" someone wondered, sympathizing with Ridge's pride.

"We'll make a cradle and carry him," Scott said and waved to a stocky, muscled cowboy to give him a hand.

Together they managed to get Ridge partially sitting up, and each slipped an arm under his legs. "Let me stand," Ridge insisted. Most of his weight was already on their shoulders, so they let his feet slide slowly to the ground. Sharon gritted her teeth as he tried to take a step. His agony dominated his expression, and his face went whiter still. He sagged against the pair.

For a second, Sharon thought he'd lost consciousness again. He didn't say a word when they scooped him up and carried him carefully to the lowered tailgate of the pickup truck. More blankets were spread across some loose hay scattered over the truck bed to make a rough mattress.

"I'll ride in back with Ridge," Sharon told her mother and crawled hurriedly into the back of the truck.

His least painful position seemed to be partly hunched over, so Sharon propped herself against the back of the cab and told Scott to lay Ridge crosswise to her. She gathered him into her arms and rested his head against her shoulder.

"It's a long ride into town," Scott warned her. "Your arms are going to get tired holding him."

"We need some blankets to wrap around him," she said, ignoring his comment, perfectly aware it was true. But her body would be a better cushion to absorb the bumpy ride than the straw bed.

"Are you all settled in back there?" Her mother had the door on the driver's side opened.

"Yes." Sharon nodded and smoothed the thick mahogany-colored hair off Ridge's forehead.

"Do you want me to come with you?" Scott vaulted over the side of the truck bed to the ground.

"Sharon and I can manage," her mother replied.

# Chapter Four

Only once did Ridge stir during the interminable ride to the hospital. Between the engine noise and the rushing wind, Sharon couldn't understand Ridge's unintelligible mutter, so she simply hugged him closer and tucked the blankets more tightly around him.

When the attendants at the emergency entrance whisked him away on a stretcher, it felt as if some part of her had been taken. Her aching arms were suddenly very empty, and her body missed the hard, punishing weight of his.

Both she and her mother were sidetracked from following the stretcher into the emergency room by a nurse. Between them, they were able to supply most of the information the admitting nurse needed for the multitude of hospital forms. Sharon found herself signing the list of valuables—jewelry, wallet, and the like—that had been removed from his person while Ridge was being wheeled to some other part of the hospital.

"X-ray," the nurse informed her with a benign smile. "Are you his fiancée?"

"No . . . just a friend," Sharon replied.

In the waiting room, Sharon and her mother each drank a cup of bitter black coffee from a dispensing machine and leafed endlessly through tattered magazines. Each time any uniformed person went by, Sharon tensed, expecting the doctor to arrive and advise them of Ridge's condition. It was the not knowing that was so terrible and wearing on the nerves—the uncertainty about the extent of his injuries.

"I didn't know it was like this," she murmured to her mother. "No one has ever been sick or hurt before—no one I knew well."

"He's going to be all right," her mother smiled in understanding.

"I keep telling myself that," Sharon managed a rueful copy of that smile.

"Can you imagine what we must look like?" Amusement suddenly gleamed in the green eyes.

Suddenly Sharon noticed her mother's floppy-brimmed cowboy hat, with wisps of hair sticking out from it like a witch's coiffure, the baggy shirt, and the scruffy, manure-stained cowboy boots. Sharon covered her mouth to smother the laugh that bubbled from her throat, aware she probably didn't look any better.

It was such a welcome release of tension that both of them started to titter, which succeeded in drawing curious looks at the pair of laughing loonys.

"Maybe we'd better find the ladies' room and make ourselves presentable," her mother suggested between laughing gasps for breath.

After Sharon had brushed the wisps of hay and dust from her jeans, tucked her shirt neatly inside the waistband, and removed her hat to comb her honey-brown hair, there was infinite improvement. Magically, her mother produced a tube of lipstick from her pocket to add the finishing touch to both their transformations.

They returned to the waiting room just as the doctor walked in. "Mrs. Powell?" He glanced questioningly at the older of the two jean-clad women with cowboy hats in hand.

"Yes," she nodded.

There was an efficient, scrubbed-clean look about the balding doctor with the shining face. Although he was slender and spare with silver wire-rimmed glasses, there was something about him that reminded Sharon of a roly-poly Santa Claus. Maybe it was his round cheeks and beaming smile.

"How is Ridge—Mr. Halliday?" she rushed the question, not giving the doctor a chance to impart the information.

"My daughter, Sharon," her mother explained when the doctor gave her a questioning look. "My husband and I own the ranch next to Mr. Halliday's. Ridge has practically been a second son to us."

"He's a very lucky man," the doctor declared. "There is evidence of some mild internal bleeding but it appears to be the result of some rather severe bruising of his internal organs rather than any perforations. You might refer to the loss as seepage—as when you scrape your skin and draw blood. Outside of that, he has a broken rib and two that are cracked."

A shiver of relief ran down Sharon's spine. "I was afraid—" she stopped and changed what she had been about to say "—he was in so much pain."

"I didn't mean to minimize the amount of pain he'll suffer," the doctor cautioned. "The bruising is very severe. It's a miracle nothing was ruptured. Naturally I'll want to keep him in the hospital a few days and monitor his condition."

"But—" It sounded more serious than he had first indicated.

He held up a calming hand. "There has been some bleeding. We want to make certain it doesn't recur—and we want to keep watch for any formation of blood clots. It's a precautionary measure."

"I see," she said, slightly reassured. "May we see him?"

The doctor nodded affirmatively. "For a few minutes. He's been given medication so he can rest."

When they entered Ridge's room and Sharon saw him, there was something incongruous about such a vital, healthy-looking male specimen lying in a hospital bed with tubes running into his veins. The fiery lights in his darkly brown hair appeared subdued in this setting. His blue eyes were such a focal point of his features that Sharon noticed the darkness of his thick brows and long lashes for the first time—because his eyes were closed.

She moved quietly to the side of the bed, unaware that her mother didn't step beyond the doorway. The lower part of his chest was strapped in white bandages, obviously support for his ribs. His bronze shoulders and arms were uncovered. Sharon lifted the blanket to draw it up around his chest and noticed the discoloration already showing through the raw, scraped redness of his stomach. And that was only the tip of the iceberg. She laid the blanket across his chest.

His eyelids flickered, then slowly opened. There was a faraway, dreamy quality to his look when Ridge focused on her. She guessed he was high on some pain-killer.

"Told you I could stand," he declared in a slurring whisper. Then his mouth curved in that reckless smile she knew so well.

"I guess I should have listened to you." She went along with whatever dream he was having.

"Damn right." His eyelids seemed to grow too heavy for him to hold open. A wince flashed across his face, proving the drug had only dulled the pain, not killed it. "Hurts."

"I know it does," Sharon agreed. "Try to get some sleep, Ridge."

His eyes were closed and she thought he had drifted into that other state. But when she started to straighten away from the bed, his hand closed on her wrist.

"Talk to me," he insisted.

"About what?" she asked quietly.

"Don't know." His head moved to one side of the pillow in some mute protest. "Never been . . . stomped on like this before. Not like this."

"You're going to be all right," she assured him, and realized he was fighting the drug, not wanting to let go of his wavering stream of consciousness.

". . . gave me something," he muttered with an angry frown. ". . . told them . . . didn't want it. . . . wouldn't listen."

"Sssh." Sharon murmured things, soothing words she might have used to calm a green horse she was training. The content was unimportant; only the steady softness of her voice mattered. Her wrist was still imprisoned in his grip, but his rough fingers had loosened their circle. He was breathing deeper, slower. Lightly she took hold of his hand loosely clasping her wrist. "You can let go now, Ridge."

His fingers uncurled as Sharon lifted her wrist free. A look of disappointment flickered across his features, then they smoothed out into an expressionless mask. She retreated from the bed and tiptoed to the door to join her mother.

"He's finally sleeping," she whispered. "We might as well go."

"Yes," her mother agreed. "I spoke to the nurse a few minutes ago. She said the doctor had left instructions to keep him sedated through the night, so there's little point in coming back this evening to see him."

"He'll need his razor, a robe, and some clean clothes. We can collect them when we go back to Latigo and I'll bring them in with me when I visit him tomorrow," Sharon murmured with a last glance at the bed and the man in it. "I'm sure he can get by until then."

To make up for her less-than-feminine appearance when Ridge had been admitted to the hospital, Sharon took extra interest in her choice of dress the next afternoon. She selected one of her favorite dresses, made of yards of soft, peach-colored material gathered in at the waist by a wide belt. It had a peasant-style, elastic neckline and long, full sleeves banded tightly at the wrist. Her throat was bare of any necklace to detract from the creamy smoothness of her skin, and her tawny hair glistened in soft curls that brushed the tops of her shoulders.

As she walked down the hospital corridor carrying Ridge's small satchel of belongings, her high-heeled sandals made attention-getting clicks. Sharon was conscious of the looks that came her way. The faint smile that touched her mouth was in remembrance of the entirely different looks she and her mother had received the day before.

All the doors to the hospital rooms were open, but when she approached Ridge's room, she saw it was shut. A nurse darted out, her expression grim, and went hurrying past Sharon toward the ward station. Before the door closed behind the nurse, Sharon caught the spate of angry voices. She quickened her stride to find out what was going on.

As she pushed the door open, she heard the tightly angry but controlled voice of a second nurse in the room. "Since you insist on being difficult, Mr. Halliday, I've sent Nurse Gaines to fetch the orderlies—"

"You can send her to hell for all I care!" Ridge snarled in response. "I told you I don't want that damned thing in my arm!"

Shutting the door quickly, Sharon moved forward a little hesitantly, trying to take lightning stock of the situation. Ridge was sitting on the edge of the hospital bed. The blanket had been pulled loose and partially wrapped around his waist, still leaving most of his legs bare. He was glaring at the flushed nurse who was glaring back.

"Do not swear at me, Mr. Halliday!" she reproved him sharply. "I am not obliged to take that kind of abuse from you or any patient!"

"Then kindly get the hell out of here," Ridge declared with a dangerously thin smile.

"Ridge!" Sharon stepped forward, drawing attention to herself. She was more than a little stunned that this man, who had the virile charm to wind this nurse around his finger, had resorted to crudeness and anger. "What is the meaning of this?" she demanded.

The look he flashed her held impatience rather than welcome. "It's about time somebody showed up," he muttered. "These damned fools took my clothes. All I've got to wear is that damned flapping gown."

The dismissive gesture of his hand turned Sharon's gaze to the crumpled hospital gown on the floor, obviously thrown there by Ridge.

"What have you got there?" His glance fell on the satchel she was carrying.

"I brought some of your things. Mom and I—"

Ridge didn't give her a chance to finish. "Did you pack me some clothes?'

"Yes—"

"Bring it here," he ordered peremptorily and extended an impatiently flicking hand to take it from her. "I'm getting out of this place," Ridge added as she brought it within his reach.

"You're in no condition—" Sharon started to pull the satchel away, but he snatched it from her before she could succeed. A rush of irritation swept through her. Like the nurse, she was fast losing her patience with him.

"All I've got is some bruises and a couple of busted ribs," he muttered. When he tried to turn slightly to open the satchel, he winced and went pale at the shafting pain that took his breath away. A moment later, he was pulling out the clean shirt and pants she'd packed for him. "Hell, I've broken my arm one day and rode the next. I'm not going to stay in here so they can keep me doped up with those damned drugs 'til I don't know up from down."

"I don't think you know up from down now," Sharon declared grimly, suspecting there was just enough of the pain-killing drug in his system for him to be numbed to the severity of his pain. "And you didn't break your arm. You are badly bruised *inside*."

But Ridge wasn't listening. The agonizing effort of getting his arms into the shirt sleeves had beaded his forehead and upper lip with perspiration. He was taking short, quick breaths to avoid aggravating the discomfort of his broken ribs. When he shook out his pants and tried to put a leg into them, the subsequent pain was so intense he groaned aloud and fell back on an elbow, swearing savagely under his breath. Involuntarily Sharon took a step toward the bed, feeling sorry for him even though she knew he was bringing it all on himself.

His half-closed eyes caught her movement. Ridge struggled to sit up again, his features whitening with the effort. "Help me get these damned pants on," he demanded through tightly clenched teeth.

"I'm not going to help you." Sharon steeled herself against the compassionate urges that tried to push her to his aid. "If you can't put your pants on, you've got no business getting out of that bed."

Her logic angered him, lighting blue flames in his eyes. "All right, dammit, I'll show you." Ridge started all over again, the strain showing in the contortions of his face as he tentatively slid a bare foot into the pants leg.

Watching him, Sharon gritted her teeth so hard they hurt. He had to keep pausing to wait for the pain to subside. By the time he managed to get both legs into the pants, sweat was trickling down his neck. He slid off the edge of the bed to pull the pants over his hips and his legs nearly buckled under him.

The nurse rushed forward to catch him, but Ridge had already braced an arm on the bed to support himself. "Mr. Halliday, please get back into bed," the nurse urged with obvious concern.

"Ridge, please," Sharon added her voice to the nurse's. It was clear to her that he was so weak and in so much pain that he could barely stand.

He shrugged off the nurse's supporting hands. "Just get away and let me get dressed." The roughness was still in his voice, but it lacked its earlier strength.

The door opened behind Sharon. She turned as the doctor came striding through, all brisk and professional. He was followed closely by the first nurse and an orderly. The cavalry was coming to the rescue, and the good doctor was leading the charge. He didn't stop until he confronted his adversary.

"What's going on here, Mr. Halliday?" he demanded sharply. "You're supposed to be in bed."

"Wrong." Ridge grabbed the bedrail for support and began inching along it.

"What do you think you're doing?" the doctor demanded with exasperation.

"I'm trying to find my damned boots so I can get out of here," Ridge muttered. "Where are they?"

"In the closet with the rest of your clothes," the doctor replied. "But you're in no condition to be released. You need at least three days of total bedrest to give your body a chance to heal itself."

"If I've got to lie in bed for three days, I'll do it back at the ranch. I'm not staying in this hospital." Clutching his stomach he staggered to the closet door. Sharon saw the doctor wave aside the orderly when he made a move to stop Ridge. Once he had his boots, Ridge more or less fell into the vinyl chair in the corner.

"It should be evident to you, Mr. Halliday, that you aren't capable of taking care of yourself." The doctor changed his confrontation tactics and attempted to reason with him. "You told me you lived alone. Who is going to fix your meals, give you your medicine, help you back and forth to the bathroom?"

The question was met initially with silence as Ridge appeared to concede that he couldn't manage alone. Then his blue gaze sought her out. "Sharon," he concluded and stuck a foot into one of the cowboy boots, seemingly oblivious to the fact he wasn't wearing socks. "She can stay at the house for a few days."

She opened her eyes a little wider at the way he took her agreement for granted, not even bothering to ask. The doctor appeared startled and glanced at Sharon as if just realizing there was a nonstaff member in the room. After a second's hesitation, he shook his head grimly.

"I'm sorry, Mr. Halliday, but I can't agree to release you from the hospital," he stated.

"I never asked you to release me," Ridge glanced at him with laughing scorn. "I'm checking myself out of here."

"If you do, I can't be held responsible for anything that might happen," the doctor warned him.

"I never asked you to be," Ridge pulled on the other boot, then remained partially hunched over, an arm folded across his stomach.

"Are you positive you want to go through with this?" the doctor persisted in the face of the patient's obvious debilitating pain.

"Yes." He made the short, one-word reply without looking up.

Resigned to accepting the decision, the doctor sighed his disapproval and glanced at the orderly. "Bring him a wheelchair."

"I don't need it." Ridge struggled to his feet, using the chair and the wall for support, and reached inside the closet for his hat.

"It's hospital rules, Mr. Halliday," the doctor informed him. "It's required by our insurance."

There was no protest from Ridge as the orderly left the room to fetch the wheelchair. His departure was closely followed by the nurses, who obviously had other duties and patients. The doctor scribbled something on a paper attached to the clipboard chart he carried, tore it off, and walked over to give it to Sharon.

"The hospital pharmacy will fill the prescription for you," he said. "He should eat nothing but soft foods the next couple of days and there should be absolutely no strenuous activity at all. I would prefer that he doesn't get out of bed, but failing that, he should be confined to the house."

Like Ridge, the doctor was taking it for granted that she was going to look after him and wasn't wasting his time giving Ridge any advice. Sharon accepted the prescription without comment.

"I know Mr. Halliday insists he doesn't want anything for the pain," the doctor continued. "But in this instance, it will be much less wearing on his system if he does take something. Rest is the best medicine for him, but it's extremely difficult to rest when you're in pain."

"I understand," Sharon nodded, then glanced up to see Ridge staggering out of the room, minus the assistance of a wheelchair.

"The man's impossible," the doctor muttered under his breath and went after him.

Silently echoing the sentiment, Sharon hurriedly gathered his dirty clothes from the closet and stuffed them into the open satchel on the bed. As she left the room, the orderly went by with the wheelchair. Ridge was halfway down the corridor, hugging the wall as he moved with obvious care.

When she caught up with the procession of patient, doctor, and orderly, the doctor's insistence that Ridge sit in the wheelchair was falling on deaf ears. He kept putting one foot in front of the other as if he didn't dare stop.

"Look, Doc—" Ridge stopped and leaned against the corner of an intersecting corridor "—I'm going to walk out of this hospital. Let this guy follow me with the wheelchair and everybody pretend I'm sitting in it."

The doctor looked at him for a long second, then swung away in disgust. "Follow him," he told the orderly and walked off muttering to himself.

Half an hour had passed by the time Ridge signed for the hospital bill and collected his personal valuables. All the while Sharon stayed quietly in the background, slipping away once to have the prescription filled. Part of her admired the grit that was carrying him through the ordeal, while the rest of her was irritated by the sheer stupidity of his refusing all help.

When they left the office to head for the hospital exit, they found the orderly had momentarily stepped away, leaving the wheelchair unattended. Ridge was free to leave the hospital on his own. Ten feet from the door, he stopped and leaned heavily against the wall. There was a grayness to his face, weakness visibly clawing at him. His gaze flicked to Sharon.

"What are you hovering around for?" he muttered roughly.

"It's the first time I've seen a real macho cowboy up close." The corners of her mouth twitched with a smile. "You're so big and brave. I thought it would be interesting to see how long you can keep it up."

"Sharon." Ridge spoke her name in a tone that tiredly appealed to her not to hassle him. He shut his eyes and let his shoulders slump. "Get the damned wheelchair."

She went back for the wheelchair and held it steady while he gingerly lowered himself into it. There was a barely stifled moan that was bitten off, then he cradled his forehead in his hand as if he lacked the strength to hold his head up. Her fingers almost touched his shoulders in a sympathetic caress, but she curled them up tightly and pulled her hand back. Her gaze lingered on the corded muscles in his neck, testimony of his pain-wracked tension.

"Now where?" She made her voice sound falsely bright and watched him stiffen.

"Home," he answered curtly.

"How do you plan to get there?" Sharon inquired innocently and tilted her head downward in smiling inquiry.

"Sharon, for God's sake, will you take me home?" Ridge demanded impatiently.

"Oh? You want me to give you a ride home," she said as if she had just discovered his intention.

"You know damned well I do," he snapped.

At that point, Sharon had had her fill of his high-handed tactics. The full skirt of her dress swirled about her legs as she moved to the front of the wheelchair. Determination ruled her expression, making her gaze just as hard and unyielding as his.

"I'm not going to take you anywhere until we settle a few things," she informed him. "First of all, you're going to do exactly as the doctor ordered."

"I'm not staying in this hospital." An instant after the firm declaration was issued, an expression flickered across his features that invisibly reached out to her with an irresistible poignancy. "I want to go home, Sharon," he murmured, a touching ache in his voice that was nearly her undoing.

"And you'll stay in bed for three days," she added the second condition.

"Two days for sure," Ridge grudgingly conceded.

"Three days," Sharon insisted. "And I'll be there to make sure you do. Do I have your word on it?" She saw his hesitation. "I'm warning you, Ridge. I'll walk away right now and leave you sitting here in this wheelchair."

An angry frown darkened his brow. "I'll call somebody else to come pick me up."

"And I'll convince them that you should stay in the hospital for your own good," she retorted, continuing to challenge him with the steadiness of her gaze. Out of the corner of her eye, she saw the orderly approaching.

A brief spark of admiration glimmered in his eyes, although his mouth remained grimly drawn. "I'm in no shape to argue with you," Ridge replied.

"I have your word?"

"Yes," he grudgingly gave in.

Her expression softened with inner relief. "Wait here while I drive the car up to the door." She smiled at the orderly who was very careful to say nothing about finding Ridge in the wheelchair. "I'll just be a minute."

# Chapter Five

The ranch appeared to be deserted when Sharon stopped the car in front of the sprawling, single-story ranch house. A golden twilight was throwing long shadows over the land and casting a yellow tinge over the buildings.

Climbing out of the car, she walked around to the passenger side to help Ridge. After he'd taken one step, she could tell he was too exhausted and weak to walk all the way to the house under his own power. She took his arm and put it around her shoulders, trying to help him without adding to his pain.

"You'd better lean on me," she advised him.

Her quick glance at his face was caught and held by his half-veiled look, so lazy and warm. There was even the suggestion of a smile around his mouth. She became conscious of the heat of his body running the length of hers, the closeness of his leanly handsome features, and the caressing warmth of his breath. A disturbance started in the pit of her stomach.

"It seems that's all I've been doing is leaning on

you," Ridge murmured while his eyes made a slow, roaming study of her upturned face. "I leaned on you all the way to the hospital—and here I am, leaning on you again."

"I know it's hard on the male ego, but you'll survive." She was having trouble breathing evenly, so she tried to make light of his comments.

"It would be easier if you were softer." Ridge shifted his position slightly to keep her shoulder bone from poking him in the side.

It was the break Sharon needed to regain control of the situation. "Come on. Let's get you inside."

With slow, measured steps, she helped him into the house, entering into it through the living room. His bedroom was the first door off the hallway. Like the rest of the house, it was Spartanly furnished. His mother had died some years ago and the house was beginning to lose the traces of a woman's touch. Except for an odd vase or two, most of the flat surfaces were bare of adornment— an indication of a man's impatience to pick up things when he dusted. Ashtrays, lamps, radios, and clocks were practically all the movable items.

Ridge sat on the edge of his bed while Sharon plumped the pillows, one atop the other, so he could rest against them. Holding himself very carefully, he shifted to lie on top of the chenille bedspread fully clothed.

"I'll go out to the car and get your things," she said and started to leave the room.

"When you come back—" his eyes remained closed as he spoke "—would you bring me a pack of cigarettes from the kitchen? They took mine away from me at the hospital. I sure could use a smoke." The last was murmured in a tired sigh.

"Sure."

Without saying more, Sharon quietly withdrew from the room and retraced her steps to the car. Returning to the house with the satchel, she paused in the spacious kitchen long enough to take a pack of cigarettes from the carton on top of the refrigerator.

When she returned to his bedroom, it didn't appear that Ridge had moved an inch from his previous position. The lines in his face seemed more deeply etched, giving the impression of pain being suppressed. There was a tinge of grayness around his compressed mouth and the pinched-in tightness of his nose. His eyelids were closed, long lashes casting shadows on the faint hollows under his eyes.

Sharon hesitated. There was no sign that he'd heard her come in. She didn't want to disturb him if he had managed to fall asleep or drifted into that in-between state that is neither sleep nor wakefulness. Rest was more vital to him than the cigarettes in her hand.

"If you're through staring, you can bring me my cigarettes." The roughness of impatience was in his voice.

Startled, it was a second before she noticed the narrow slits of his eyes, observing her while they appeared to be closed. Recovering, she walked calmly to the side of the bed.

"I thought you might be asleep," she said.

"If I was, I suppose you were going to wake me like those damned nurses, so you could take my pulse and check my temperature," Ridge grumbled.

"I'll bet they enjoyed sticking a thermometer in your mouth just for the pleasure of shutting you up," Sharon countered, and observed the slight widening of his eyes to more than slits.

"It's wonderful that you're so understanding," he murmured with dry sarcasm.

"I understand, all right," she assured him. "You feel rotten, so you behave rottenly to everyone around you. Misery loves company."

He shut his eyes and made no comment to her remark. "Light me a cigarette." As an obvious afterthought, he added an explanation to the demand. "Right now, the pain's bearable and I don't want to move."

Sharon shook a cigarette from the pack, then picked up the book of matches from the bedside table to light it. "Shall I smoke it for you, too?" she asked and blew out the match flame along with a stream of smoke from her mouth.

"Very funny," Ridge murmured. "Why don't you pretend it's a thermometer."

With his eyes shut, Ridge didn't see her amused smile as Sharon reached over and placed the lit cigarette between his lips. Her fingers briefly touched his mouth before she drew them away. They tingled slightly from the intimate contact with his smooth, hard lips.

As she straightened, she noticed the cautious way he lifted his hand to take the cigarette from his mouth after he'd taken a short drag. Even then, he winced as if jarred by the careful motion.

"Where would you like me to set the ashtray?" Sharon realized that it would be too painful for Ridge to twist himself around to use it if she left it on the bedside table.

"Just somewhere within reach," he said, then added hastily, "but not on my stomach. It hurts to have anything touch it—even these clothes."

"Do you want me to help you take them off?" she offered, as she placed the ashtray on the bed next to him and half-turned from the bed in the direction of the chest of drawers and the clothes closet. "Last night, Mom and I looked for a pair of pajamas and a robe to take to the hospital, but we couldn't find any. Where do you keep them?'

Ridge started to laugh, but the bruised muscles in his stomach must have screamed a protest because it ended in a groan. When he finally answered, his tight voice was heavily threaded with suppressed pain.

"I haven't owned a pair of pajamas since I was ten," he told her. "And as for a robe . . . when you live in an all-male household, you don't need one." A smile deepened the corners of his mouth at the stunned look on her face. "Do you still want to play nurse?" Ridge mocked.

She recovered instantly. "For heaven's sake, I'm not a schoolgirl anymore," she flashed in annoyance, irritated with herself—and with him for drawing attention to her brief moment of self-consciousness. "I'm not likely to be shocked by the sight of a man's body. I do have a brother."

"In that case, I would like these clothes off," he acknowledged, still watching her with a challenging gleam in his eyes.

Sharon didn't falter for a second. "Then I'll take these." She picked up the ashtray she'd just set on the bed and removed the partially smoked cigarette from his hand. "Can you sit up by yourself, or do you need some help?"

"I can manage."

His stiff and stilted movements were such a marked contrast to his usual effortless and fluid motion that Sharon couldn't help noticing it. But she stood back and let Ridge take as much time as he needed to sit up and swing his legs over the side of the bed.

"The boots first," she said and knelt down to tug them off.

Without socks to ease the friction, it wasn't easy. She closed her ears to the half-smothered, grunting sounds of pain that came from him. When both boots had been removed, she set them next to the dresser. Ridge already had his shirt half unbuttoned, so she unfastened the last few and eased one arm out of the shirt sleeve. After that, it was a simple matter of slipping it off the other.

As he edged off the bed to stand up so his pants could be taken off, Sharon avoided meeting his gaze. She was very careful when she unfastened his pants so her hands wouldn't touch the badly discolored flesh of his stomach. Her hands were steady and sure as they inched the pants over his hips and slid them quickly down his legs. The white material of his jockey shorts filled her peripheral vision, but she concentrated on her task.

Ridge lowered himself onto the edge of the bed and the pants slid onto the floor. His bare legs were in front of her. For an instant, she let her gaze linger on the silken-fine hair covering them. She had never found hairy men very attractive, but Ridge wasn't covered with a furry, dark mat.

As she straightened to hang up his clothes, she caught his eye. Amusement danced openly in the blue irises. It instantly made her conscious of the warmth in her cheeks. She had been so positive she had been a model of indifference at the sight of his lean and muscled body that she hadn't been aware of the building heat in her cheeks.

"Don't look now, nurse, but you're blushing," Ridge informed her in a deeply resonant voice as he tried very hard not to laugh because it would hurt too much.

Denying it would be foolish. She picked up the burning cigarette from the ashtray and passed it to him. "Smoke your cigarette."

"—and shut up?" An arching brow queried whether that was the rest of her suggestion.

"And shut up," Sharon agreed with a sweetly angry look and walked to the closet to put away his clothes.

"Sorry," Ridge said. "I guess it wasn't fair to tease you."

No suitable reply occurred to her, but she swallowed her anger. It served no purpose except to give him more fuel. Her expression was calm when she turned back to the bed.

"I'll be in the kitchen if you need me," she said and exited the room.

In the sunny yellow kitchen with its shiny white cabinets and windows facing to the east to catch the light from a rising sun, Sharon halted her hasty retreat from Ridge's bedroom and paused to calm her shaky nerves. There were bound to be more intimate moments like this last one during the next few days. She was going to be in constant contact with him—figuratively and literally—so she might as well come to grips with it and stop turning it into a sexual encounter every time. She was here to take care of him—as a family friend and neighbor—and that was all!

Her breathing returned to a more normal rate. A corner of her mouth lifted in a wry semblance of a smile turned inward. With considerable more aplomb, Sharon was remembering Ridge's testy behavior. It was amazing how one man could be so infuriatingly difficult—and so damned sexy at the same time!

A telephone extension was mounted on the kitchen wall. Sharon crossed the room and lifted the receiver to dial her parents' number so she could advise them of the changed situation. Her mother answered on the fourth ring.

After Sharon had informed her about Ridge's condition and explained her subsequent decision to take care of him at the ranch when he stubbornly refused to stay in the hospital, there was a few seconds of silence on the other end of the line.

"Under the circumstances, I don't see what other decision you could have made," her mother finally concluded with a trace of a sigh.

"Ridge is certainly in no condition to take care of himself," Sharon reaffirmed. Neither of them directly alluded to her past infatuation for Ridge, but it was behind every word that was spoken—a silent reminder to proceed with caution. "Would you pack me some clothes for the next few days?"

"I'll have Scott run them over to the ranch. He was planning to go to the hospital to see Ridge tonight anyway. Oh, I almost forgot," her mother declared suddenly. "Andy Rivers phoned. I told him you'd be home later tonight. He's going to call back. What do you want me to tell him?"

Sharon hesitated. It was funny, but when she tried to conjure up an image of his face, it was all fuzzy and out of focus. Ridge's overpowering personality was to blame for that. Friendship had been the mainstay of her relations with the young geologist—for both parties. But even that feeling had dimmed dangerously in the few short days dominated by Ridge or thoughts of him.

"Have Andy call me here," Sharon stated firmly, determined the Latigo Ranch wasn't going to become a desert island with only herself and Ridge as occupants. Retaining contact with the outside world was essential. "Was there anything else?"

After exchanging a few more words, Sharon rang

off. She had just begun investigating the contents of the kitchen cupboards to find something soft and easily digestible for Ridge to eat when there was a knock at the back door.

An incoming ranch hand had noticed the car and came to inquire about Ridge's condition, thinking that someone from the Powell family had been to the hospital to see him. After Sharon explained that Ridge had discharged himself from the hospital, the cowboy went in to see him.

While he visited with Ridge, Sharon went back into the kitchen to prepare a meal. The cupboard had yielded a can of creamed split pea with ham soup and a jar of applesauce. Beyond that, she had to improvise. With a dish towel tied around her waist to protect her peach-colored dress, Sharon peeled potatoes to boil and mash and scrounged around to find some kind of tray to serve the meal on while the potatoes were cooking.

The ranch hand was still in the room when Sharon carried in Ridge's supper, using the top part of a TV tray she'd found tucked away in the pantry. From the little conversation she'd overheard before entering the room, she had the impression Ridge had been grilling the man on the amount of work that had been done the last two days. The cowboy seemed glad of her interruption and the excuse to leave.

"I'll tell Hobbs what you said. He'll be gettin' back with you," the cowboy said as he backed out of the room.

Sharon paused beside the bed with the tray in

her hands. "How do you want to do this?" she asked. "Do you want to sit up and cushion the tray on your lap with a pillow? Or shall I feed you? I've had a lot of practice playing airplane with Tony. The spoon is the airplane and your mouth is the hangar it flies into."

"I'll feed myself," Ridge replied, unamused by her mocking suggestion.

Flattening his hands on the mattress, he levered himself into a more upright sitting position. He went white with the effort, briefly baring his teeth against the ensuing pain before clamping his mouth tightly shut. Sharon pretended not to notice, aware he didn't like the thought of anyone, especially a woman, seeing him so weak that he could barely sit up by himself. Neither would he welcome any show of sympathy, so she partially turned aside to set the tray on the bedside table and get a spare pillow from the closet to lay across his sore stomach.

When she returned to the bed with a pillow in hand, his gaze had narrowed on the tray of food. It turned sharply to her face.

"That's the same junk they tried to feed me in the hospital," he accused.

"The doctor said no solid food for a few days— and you promised to follow his orders," Sharon reminded him, letting her glance slide to meet his eyes while she gently laid the pillow on his lap and tried not to take too much notice of the sinewy, muscled width of his bare chest above his bandaged ribs. She placed the tray on the pillow, making sure it was balanced before letting go of the sides. "Now eat," she ordered and straightened to study the distaste that showed on his face as Ridge viewed the meal before him. "Maybe your disposition will improve with some food in your stomach."

The corners of his mouth were pulled in grimly with dislike. "I want something I can sink my teeth into," he muttered.

"You'll have to content yourself with snapping at me," Sharon retorted.

The upward sweep of his gaze took in the towel tied around her waist, the shallow rise and fall of her breasts beneath the peasant-style bodice of her dress, and the creamy smoothness of her throat and neck before stopping when it reached her face. A lazily seductive gleam entered his blue eyes.

"I might enjoy taking a bite out of you," Ridge murmured.

Sharon didn't immediately release the breath she drew in, her pulse accelerating under his disturbing look. It was a full second before she managed a brief laugh to break the spell over her senses.

"Don't you know you aren't supposed to bite the hand that feeds you?" she mocked him. "You might discover that I bite back."

"I hope so," he drawled in answer, a slow smile edging his mouth.

The room suddenly felt very warm. "If you'll excuse me, I think I'll go fix myself something to eat. You may not be hungry, but I am." Sharon wanted to leave before she was drawn into another word battle laced with sexual overtones. "I'll come back for the tray when you're finished."

As she turned to leave, her eye caught the change in his expression out of her side vision. The glinting, roguish light faded from his eyes and his features once again showed the gray pallor of constant pain. The suggestive looks and remarks he'd passed had provided Ridge with a mental distraction from his suffering. He wasn't really interested in her, and she'd do well to remember that.

Word that Ridge was home from the hospital had evidently spread quickly throughout the ranch. Within half an hour after the cowboy left, the foreman Hobbs knocked at the door. When Sharon showed him into the bedroom, Ridge insisted she take away the tray. It looked as if no more than a couple of bites had been taken of each item.

Sharon's mouth thinned with displeasure when she saw how little he'd eaten, but she knew she'd never accomplish anything by admonishing him in front of his foreman for not eating more. She'd grown up with the macho egos of western men and knew that such a remark, regardless of the genuine concern behind it, would be considered as undermining their authority. So she simply flashed him a disapproving look and silently left the room carrying the tray of food.

There was a steady stream of visitors throughout the evening. Her brother, Scott, was the last to come, arriving as Sharon finished washing the dishes from the two separate meals she'd cooked. He'd brought the suitcase her mother had packed for her. While Scott went in to visit Ridge, Sharon took her case into the bedroom next to Ridge's to unpack and settle in.

Like all the rest of the rooms, this one was minus any frills. Her silk nightgown and matching robe appeared out of place when she laid them on the plain blue chenille spread at the end of the bed. After she had arranged her cosmetics and toiletries in the private bathroom adjoining the bedroom, she noticed her reflection in the mirrored medicine chest and realized she was still wearing the dish-towel apron.

As she retraced her steps from the bedroom to the hallway, heading for the kitchen, she worked to loosen the knotted towel ends behind her back. Scott emerged from the open door to Ridge's room just as she went by. Her glance went to him in surprise.

"Are you leaving already?" Sharon doubted that her brother had been in the room more than twenty minutes.

"I've gotta get home." His voice was deliberately loud so that Ridge would hear his answer as he fell into step with her. Immediately it dropped to a more private level. "Didn't the doctor give him anything to take for the pain?"

"I have a prescription in my purse, but I don't know if he'll take it," she said.

"Give it to him whether he wants it or not," her brother advised. "I was in there gritting my teeth for him. He'll never get any rest at this rate unless he passes out."

"I'll see that he gets it," she nodded and slowed her steps as they neared the back door.

"Mom said to call if you need anything." Scott reached for the knob, turning it. "One of us will be over tomorrow night."

"Okay." Her smile faded as he left the house, her expression becoming serious with concern.

Before going to Ridge's room, Sharon stopped in the kitchen and absently laid the towel on the counter near her purse. Opening her purse, she took out the bottle of pills and read the written instructions on the prescription label.

"Sharon!" The interior walls partially muffled the demanding call from Ridge.

Leaving the pill bottle on the counter, she moved quickly in the direction of his room. "Coming!" she raised her voice in answer.

A thin, smoke-blue haze hung in the upper air near the ceiling when she entered. Ridge was propped in the same position as earlier in the evening, but there seemed to be a marked deterioration in his condition. His features were decidedly haggard and drawn and the glitter in his eyes seemed tortured. There was an occasional, very faint tremor in various parts of his body. Sharon had the distinct impression that he wanted to writhe with pain, but it hurt him too much to move. The last of the hospital medication had worn off, leaving him without any barrier to screen out the pain.

"Bring me another pack of cigarettes." He wadded up the empty pack and added it to the mound of cigarette butts in the ashtray. "And empty this."

"You're smoking too much," she criticized automatically, aware that he was using smoking as a distraction.

"I don't need any lectures, just a pack of cigarettes," he retorted irritably.

"What you need is rest," Sharon stated. She walked to the bed, took away the ashtray and emptied it into the wastebasket by the dresser, but didn't carry it back to the bed. "I'll bring you a couple of the pain pills the doctor prescribed. They'll help you sleep."

"I don't want any of those damned drugs," Ridge flashed angrily but in a tightly controlled voice. "That's why I checked out of the hospital."

Turning, she faced the bed, her hands moving up to rest on her hips in a challenging stance. "Still determined to tough it out, are you?" she chided him for being so foolish.

There was a moment of silence during which his hard, level gaze held her eyes. "Are you going to get my cigarettes or not?" he demanded.

"No," Sharon replied smoothly. "If you want another pack, get out of bed and get it yourself." If he tried, Sharon was positive he'd collapse before he reached the hall.

His mouth tightened into a line that matched the hardness of his flinty blue eyes, indicating he suspected the same. "You're enjoying this, aren't you?" Ridge muttered.

"Immensely," she assured him and hid the wrenching concern she actually felt. As he passed a hand over his face, she noticed the faint tremor of his fingers. She relented from her attitude of indifference and suggested, "Hot milk is supposed to relax a person and help them fall asleep. Shall I heat some for you?"

Ridge started to reject the offer, then changed his mind. "If I promise to drink it, will you bring me a pack of cigarettes?"

"That's blackmail," Sharon accused.

"Yes." He smiled briefly, the movement accentuating the tautness of his mouth.

After a second's hesitation, she smiled and uttered a surrendering sigh. "You've got a deal," she agreed.

In the kitchen, Sharon poured milk into a pan and set the pan on a stove burner. While it was heating, she shook two prescription pills out of the bottle and placed them on a square of wax paper, then used a rolling pin to grind them into a white powder. After she added it to the scalded milk, she sipped a spoonful. The bitterness pinched her lips together. To disguise it, Sharon quickly added a generous amount of chocolate syrup and then plopped a marshmallow into the cup.

With a fresh pack of cigarettes in one hand and the mug of hot chocolate in the other, she returned to the bedroom. "I changed the hot milk to hot cocoa. I thought you'd drink it with less fuss," she announced as she entered.

"You can set it on the stand," Ridge instructed, referring to the chocolate and reaching for the cigarettes.

"No." She held the pack of cigarettes behind her back. "Drink the cocoa first, then you can have the cigarettes." She gave him the cup and watched him take the first drink, unconsciously holding her breath while she waited for his reaction.

"You got a little carried away with the chocolate, didn't you?" he remarked.

"Did I put in too much?" Sharon inquired innocently.

"It's all right." He took another drink. "It's just a little strong." He slid a sideways look at her. "I suppose I have to drink all of it before you give me the cigarettes."

"Yes—to the very last drop." She didn't want any medication settling to the bottom of the cup. As he lifted the cup to his mouth again, Sharon walked to the dresser and retrieved the ashtray. After several more swallows, Ridge tilted the cup to drain it dry.

"There, I've been a good boy. Now, how about lighting me a cigarette?" The haggardness of his features seemed more pronounced as he lowered the cup to the bed. The upward curve of his mouth was closer to a smiling wince.

Sharon lighted one and traded it for the empty mug in his hand. Ridge puffed on it, unable to inhale the smoke too deeply. The nicotine didn't appear to offer him much comfort or relief. Sharon moved toward the door.

"Where are you going?" Ridge stopped her with his question.

"The kitchen, so I can clean up the mess I left."

"Oh." His glance fell to the burning tip of his cigarette, then quickly skipped back to her, his pain-bright eyes silent in their appeal. "When you're finished, would you come back and talk to me?"

It was a request to have his mind distracted from the incessant messages of pain traveling through his nervous system being expressed, not a desire for her company. Sharon reminded herself of that as she smiled.

"Sure." For both their sakes, she hoped the medication worked quickly.

It only took her a few minutes to rinse the cup, pan, and utensils she'd used and to straighten up the kitchen. When she returned to Ridge's room, the cigarette had been crushed out in the ashtray and his head was resting against the headboard of the bed, his eyes closed. He opened them a slit to acknowledge his awareness of her presence in the room but otherwise didn't move.

"Instead of talking, I think you should see if you can't go to sleep," Sharon suggested quietly.

"Yeah." It was a tired agreement. Ridge stirred, as if intending to change his position, then subsided onto the pillows. "I can't even lie down by myself." The remark was inadvertently muttered aloud, an admission that he couldn't withstand the additional pain produced by movement. "Would you help me lie down?" Grudgingly he made the request of her.

"Of course." She suspected that his bruised stomach muscles simply couldn't withstand the strain of slowly lowering his torso into a prone position.

At the side of the bed, Sharon lifted the full skirt of her dress out of the way so that she could rest a knee on the mattress to give herself leverage. Bending over Ridge, she slipped one arm behind him while she removed the pillows propping him up with her other hand.

# Chapter Six

Although Ridge tried to help when Sharon began to lower him gently onto the mattress, his strength and capacity were severely limited, and she was obliged to support the bulk of his weight. When he was finally lying flat, she found herself in a ridiculous position, with her arm pinned under him while she leaned over him, trying very hard not to touch his sore ribs or stomach accidentally. She made a wriggling attempt to free her arm, without success.

"Can you lift up just a little so I can get my arm out?" she asked, out of breath from the exertion.

His face looked ghastly white under its tan, and beads of perspiration had gathered on his upper lip. "Wait a minute." His voice was unnaturally thin and taut.

Despite the care she'd taken, the change of positions had obviously released a whole new series of stabbing pains. Sharon made no reply as she patiently waited for the fresh throbbings within him to dull. In the meantime, she had a hand braced on the pillow by his head and her arm trapped beneath his weight while her face hovered above the point of his shoulder near the slashing angle of his jaw. His eyes remained closed, black lashes lying thick and roughly spiked together.

The color returned slowly to his face as his breathing began to return to its normal steadiness. Lifting his lashes, Ridge looked at her through half-closed eyes. Their blueness held a mixture of relief at the subsiding pain and self-mocking chagrin at his weakness.

"Are you okay?" she asked, now that he seemed to have recovered.

"Yeah." His mouth twisted wryly. "I never realized how impossible it is to move without using your stomach muscles."

"That's why the only cure for you is complete rest. If you had stayed in the hospital, they have beds that crank up and down." She was becoming cramped in her position, half-leaning over and half-lying down.

"I thought nurses took care of their patients without complaint," Ridge chided.

"I'm not a nurse." Sharon wiggled her arm under his back to remind him she was still pinned by his heavy weight.

"No, that isn't a uniform, is it?" he said with a slow perusal of her dress and the soft folds of its full skirt falling over him and the bed. "What color is it?"

"Peach." In her position, the peasant-style neckline was threatening to expose a bare shoulder.

"Nice." He fingered the hem of her skirt, which was closest to his hand. "Soft," he remarked on the texture of the fabric, then his half-closed gaze slid back to her.

She felt the disturbing difference in his attention, something that had been bred by the forced intimacy of their positions and that had been growing ever since. This sudden tension seemed to snatch at her breath and heighten her senses. She was conscious of so many things all at once, the smell of him tinged with hospital antiseptic and tobacco smoke, the sight of the throbbing blue vein in his throat, and the touch of his calloused hand rasping over the smoothness of her nylon-clad thigh.

"You should wear dresses more often." His voice was pitched low and velvety husky. "I never noticed your legs until today. You have beautiful legs."

"Really." Sharon tried to sound calmly indifferent, but her voice came out all thick and disturbed, throbbing with the attraction she was feeling.

"Really," Ridge repeated her response with mocking emphasis. "Do you mind that I noticed your legs? You seemed quite interested in mine earlier."

She chose to ignore his comment. "This is very uncomfortable. Would you mind moving so I can get my arm out?"

"I think I would," he replied thoughtfully.

His hand ceased its absent stroking of her leg and came away from beneath her skirt to slide up her back and tunnel under the weight of her hair. Sharon resisted the slight pressure his fingers exerted to move her closer to his mouth.

"Ridge, let me go." There was a trace of exasperation in her voice as if her patience with him had been pushed to the limit.

"Careful," he warned when her resistance started to take on a more physical aspect. "You wouldn't hurt a guy when he was down, would you?"

"When it's you, I might," Sharon retorted, but she couldn't bring herself to inflict any additional pain on him, unintentionally or not.

"No, you wouldn't." Ridge was very confident about that as she let herself be coerced into seeking contact with his mouth.

He rubbed it over her lips, warming them with his touch and his breath. She found herself enjoying just the feel of her sensitive lips moving against his, nuzzling and exploring in a purely sensuous fashion. His hand slid down to the side of her waist, no longer possessing the strength to ensure that she maintained the intimate contact. It wasn't necessary.

Of its own accord, the mutual investigation grew into a long, breathless kiss. The thudding of her heart sounded loudly in her ears when Sharon finally drew an inch away from him. She felt the light touch of his finger under her jaw. It glided to the point of her chin, then shifted to trace the outline of her lips, still warm from his possession of them.

"You have the softest lips," he murmured.

The lift of his chin invited them back. The last kiss had been marked by gentle seduction, but this time Sharon sensed a frustrated urgency in the moving pressure of his mouth. His hand dug into her waist with unconscious force, as if he wanted to pull her into his embrace and dared not. She, too, wanted to relax against him and feel the hard contours of his muscled body against hers, but she held herself rigidly away from him. Her weight on his broken ribs and badly bruised stomach would cause more pain than pleasure. Before the ache inside became any stronger, Sharon broke off the kiss.

"It's no good, Ridge. You'd better let me up." Her voice was softly taut with things better left unsaid.

"I ought to make you stay here all night," he retorted thickly. "'Beware of Greeks bearing gifts.'"

Sharon didn't see what one thing had to do with another. "What?"

His gaze narrowed at her briefly and then moved to the shoulder bared by the drooping neckline of her dress. He shifted it back into its proper position, then let his finger hook itself on the elastic neckline while it traveled to the middle front until it rested against the slope of her breast, creating a tingle.

"You put something in that cocoa, didn't you?" Ridge accused.

After a brief hesitation, she openly admitted her trick. "Yes. You needed something to dull the pain, so I ground up two of the pills the doctor prescribed for you and dissolved them in the milk."

"I thought I felt odd," he muttered.

For some reason, his remark struck her wrong, hardening all her sympathies into stone. Without caring any more whether it hurt him, she jerked her arm out from beneath him. Remorse flashed for an instant at his involuntary grunt of pain. Already she was pushing off the bed onto the floor.

"You didn't have to be so rough," he snapped.

"I thought you were a big, tough guy," Sharon countered, with a hint of mockery. "It only hurts for a little while."

"All that honey and sweetness has turned to vinegar, hasn't it?" His mouth thinned. "What's the matter? Are you sore at yourself for kissing me?"

"Rest is the cure for what ails you," she retorted. "Not sex."

"Is that part of the doctor's orders?" Ridge mocked.

"No. It's mine," she flared.

The sudden ringing of the phone on the bedside table startled Sharon. She whirled to face the noisy interruption, then quickly took a breath to calm her jangled nerves before reaching to pick up the receiver.

"Latigo Ranch." Her voice was unnaturally low but steady when she answered.

"Hello?" An uncertain male voice came back, vaguely familiar, but Sharon just thought it was some neighboring rancher calling to find out how Ridge was doing. "Is . . . is this Sharon?"

"Yes." Her forehead became knitted with a small frown.

"It didn't sound like you," the voice replied with relief. As if sensing from her blank silence that she still hadn't identified him, the caller eliminated the problem. "This is Andy . . . Andy Rivers. Your mother told me where you were when I called the house a few minutes ago."

"Yes, I told her to have you phone me here," Sharon remembered belatedly.

"Who is it?" Ridge demanded from the bed.

She threw a glance at him, not wanting to carry on an essentially personal conversation with Andy in his presence. "Just a minute Andy," she said into the phone, then clamped a hand over the mouthpiece while she answered Ridge's question. "It's for me."

"Andy, the oil man boyfriend." Ridge had caught the name and connected it, a trace of sarcasm in his disparaging tone.

Sharon wanted to snap back some kind of denial, both at his description and at his tone, but Andy was probably calling long distance. She didn't want to keep him waiting on the line while she argued with Ridge.

"I'm going to take the call in the kitchen," she informed him stiffly. "Would you hang up the receiver here after I've picked up the one in there?"

"Talk to him here," Ridge challenged. "Or are you too embarrassed to whisper love words in his ear while I'm listening?"

"It's a personal call, which I wish to conduct in privacy." She refused to let him goad her into taking the call in his room. She took her hand away from the mouthpiece and spoke into the phone again. "Hold on a second, Andy, while I switch to the extension in the kitchen." Not trusting Ridge, she added, "If we *accidentally* get disconnected in the process, call me back."

After she had passed the receiver to Ridge, she moved the phone within easy reaching distance so he could hang it up once she was on the extension. He eyed her coolly.

Without waiting for Ridge to continue his attempt to incite an argument, Sharon left the room and hurried to the wall phone in the kitchen. She picked up the receiver and tried to force the tension from her body.

"Hello, Andy." She waited until she heard his puzzled but affirmative response before she said to Ridge, "You can hang up the phone now." There was a long moment before she heard the click of the extension going dead. It was funny, but she didn't feel as relieved as she had expected. "Sorry to keep you waiting on the line for so long, Andy, but I . . . just gave Ridge some pills to help him sleep. I didn't want my conversation with you to disturb him."

"Your mother mentioned something about Halliday having an accident. What happened?" he inquired.

Sharon retold the story as briefly as she could and made an even sketchier explanation of how and why she had volunteered to look after Ridge in his home. But he didn't seem to think it was either unusual or improper. Sharon smiled at herself, wondering why on earth she had thought Andy would be upset or possibly jealous. A guilty conscience, she supposed.

Finally the conversation came around to the reason for his call. "I'm going to be in town over the weekend. I thought we might take in a show together Saturday night."

"It sounds great," Sharon accepted the indirect invitation. "Ridge should be up and around by then, so I'll probably be home. Why don't you call on Saturday to be sure?"

"I'll do that," Andy agreed. "If you aren't there, I'll understand the movie date is cancelled."

"No." She rushed to eliminate that conclusion, not entirely sure why she didn't want to accept an easy excuse. "Even if I'm still at Latigo, we can go to the movies. Scott can come over and visit with Ridge if he isn't in any shape to be left alone."

"As long as you're sure that isn't going to create any conflict, I'll see you Saturday night around six," he said.

"Just be sure to call first to find out where I am," Sharon reminded him.

Goodbyes were exchanged and they rang off. Sharon bit thoughtfully at the inside of her lip as she turned from the wall phone and moved slowly in the direction of Ridge's bedroom. She had the uncomfortable feeling that she was trying to use the Saturday-night date with Andy as some kind of shield—as if it could protect her from the long-held attraction she had for Ridge. If that's what she was doing, it was both childish and cowardly.

"Did you and lover boy have an argument?" His taunting voice halted her when she would have walked past his doorway.

"No. Andy was calling long distance." Or so she had presumed. Ridge's earlier comment prompted her to add, "So we kept it short and sweet."

His face bore a disgruntled look. "I guess I owe you an apology for the way I snapped at you earlier—and for some of my remarks." Apology didn't come easily to him, and it showed in the tautness of his wording. Perhaps it meant something because it was honest, rather than an insincere attempt to smooth over an argument. "It doesn't seem to take much to rub me the wrong way—not the way I'm hurting. It isn't much of an excuse but—I do appreciate you staying here to look after me. I sure as hell can't do it myself."

Not five minutes ago, Sharon had been prepared to stay angry at him for the duration. But all that resentment was fading in the wake of his apology and his grudging admission that he needed her.

"Apology accepted, Grumpy." A small smile touched her mouth.

A glint of humor entered his drug-tired eyes. "If I'm Grumpy, you must be Doc. And those pills you put in my cocoa must be Snow White. Either that or they were the poisoned apple."

"Why don't you stop fighting it and close your

eyes?" suggested Sharon. "You need the sleep. I'll be in the next room. Just call out if you need anything."

"Okay," he said and let his eyelids drift shut, the potent drug taking its effect.

Unfortunately, Sharon didn't find it so easy to fall asleep. After she'd taken a bath and climbed into bed, sleep eluded her. The day had been so packed with activity that she couldn't seem to bring it to an end, despite the late evening hour.

The combination of a busy day, a strange bed, and the knowledge of Ridge sleeping in the next room denied her sleep until sometime after midnight. Even then, Sharon slept lightly, alert to any sound. Twice she went to check on Ridge in the middle of the night, positive she'd heard him. Both times he was sleeping deeply, and Sharon went back to crawl into her own bed to make another attempt to do the same.

Exhaustion had taken her into a dreamless slumber when a loud crash shattered her sleep. She sat bolt upright and listened. The yellowing streaks of dawn were spreading through the grayness of the sky outside her bedroom windows. Sharon was still trying to decide whether she'd actually heard something or merely imagined it again when a muffled curse came through the wall between the two bedrooms.

Sharon grabbed for her jade-green robe as she scurried out of bed and went flying into the hallway. She was frantically trying to tie the sash as she reached the open door and stopped to stare at Ridge. Half-naked, wearing only his jockey shorts, he was holding onto the footrail of his bed.

"What are you doing out of bed? Why didn't you call me?" she demanded angrily and hurried to his side without waiting for an answer. Taking his arm, she draped it around her shoulders so she could help him back to bed.

"I made it this far. I can make it the rest of the way," Ridge grumbled and pulled his arm away. To prove his point, he began hopping along the edge of the mattress until he was at the middle of the bed.

"What's wrong with your foot?" Sharon frowned.

"I stubbed my toe on a corner of the dresser," he muttered. His answer explained the noise that had awakened her. As he sat on the edge of the bed, he made all sorts of faces in an effort to hold in any vocal expression of pain. Lying down was a different thing. He threw her an irritated look. "Don't just stand there. Help me."

As she helped him lie flat, she was careful not to get her arm trapped again. She lifted the weight of her sleep-tousled hair away from the side of her face. "How did you manage to get out of bed without help?"

"As the old saying goes—it was as easy as falling out of bed. Nothing to it," Ridge insisted dryly, his features smoothing out as the pain subsided. "What time is it? It looks like it must be close to five in the morning."

Sharon glanced at the alarm clock on the table. "It will be in another ten minutes."

"Good. I'm starved. How about fixing me some breakfast?" he asked.

She really wanted to crawl back into bed and get some of the sleep she'd missed, but she stifled a yawn. "I guess it's time to be getting up," she agreed wearily.

"I'll have three fried eggs over easy, hash-browns, and a couple of rashers of bacon," Ridge ordered. "Toast and jelly, too. Juice and milk and coffee."

"You can have oatmeal with either applesauce or mashed bananas, or hot milk with toast," she informed him. "The juice, milk, and coffee part of your order is okay."

He gave her a not too pleased look. "How long do I have to eat this baby food?"

"Until you stop acting like one and start doing what you're told." The faintly barbed exchange was chasing away her tiredness. Mental alertness was always essential around Ridge.

"Is that right?" Behind the mockery of his vague smile there was a glint of amusement in his expression. "Is that why you mix my medicine into my food—the same way you would with a baby?"

"If the bootie fits—" Sharon murmured.

Ridge chuckled, although not too vigorously because of the pain in his ribs and stomach. "I'll have oatmeal and applesauce. No pills, please—at least not for the time being. I don't want to become dependent on them. If I do have to end up taking them, I want them on the side with a glass of water."

She smiled her approval. "You don't like being called a baby, do you? I wouldn't worry about it. All men are big babies, no matter how tough they act."

"And where did you glean that bit of priceless information?" he said mockingly.

"From years of observing my father and my brother. The only difference between men and little boys is the size and the price of their toys," she chimed. "They like being spoiled and having their own way."

"What do women like?" Ridge gingerly crooked an arm under his head, elevating it a few inches and changing the angle of his view.

"Now that would be telling," Sharon laughed.

"From my limited observation of the opposite sex—" he began to make his own guess, watching her with lazy interest, "—I'd say they enjoy mothering—which includes everything from spoiling to giving orders."

"I don't think I would say that," she hedged against agreeing with his answer.

His mouth crooked into a half-smile. "Look at yourself. You like the feeling of power you have over me—telling me what I'm going to eat and giving me my medicine even if it involves tricking me. A part of you is glad that I'm laid up, because it makes me dependent on you. So you can be nice and loving—or stern and commanding."

The more she thought about his observation, the

more accurate it sounded. Sharon wasn't sure that she liked it. Even though she had accused him of liking to be waited on, she had never thought of herself as liking to wait on him.

"Maybe it's true," she conceded. "Any maybe it's simply human nature—on both parts."

"How come you don't want to admit that you like telling me what to do because you know I'm in no condition to do anything about it?" Ridge challenged with a taunting gleam in his eyes.

"It's definitely a unique feeling," she admitted, although she was uncomfortable admitting to anything beyond that.

"And you like it?" he persisted.

"I suppose I do." Her chin lifted a fraction of an inch, tilting to a challenging angle. "It's nice to have the upper hand once in awhile." Since he claimed she did in this instance, Sharon took advantage of her position. "Stay in bed and don't try to get out by yourself while I'm fixing your breakfast."

"Yes, ma'am." His submissive reply was deliberately mocking, denying the obedience and respect implied by the words.

"I think I liked you better when you were Grumpy," Sharon declared in a parting shot as she turned to leave the room.

"Just like a woman." Ridge's taunting voice trailed after. "You like to have the last word."

A vague sense of irritation threaded through her nerves as Sharon swept into the hallway. There was always an element of truth in generalizations. So to that degree, the things Ridge had said were true. It simply wasn't the whole truth.

She had the feeling that she hadn't handled the conversation very well. She had started out in control, but somewhere it had shifted into his hands. Shaking her head, Sharon realized it was silly to make a contest out of every conversation she had with Ridge. There was no need to feel she had to compete with him at every turn. There might be times when she needed to defend herself against one of his advances—and that was only because her heart was vulnerable where he was concerned, not because she was physically afraid of him.

After fixing his breakfast, Sharon added a second cup of freshly brewed coffee for herself to the tray and carried it to the bedroom. A few minutes were spent helping Ridge maneuver into a sitting position before she could arrange the tray on his lap. He noticed the second cup of coffee as she took it from the tray.

An eyebrow lifted in querying arch. "Aren't you eating breakfast?"

"Not now. I'll fix myself something after I've washed and dressed." She sipped at the coffee, cupping the mug in both hands.

There was a slight narrowing of his eyes, although they continued to shine with a blue gleam. His glance flicked from the bowl of oatmeal on the tray to her face.

"I suppose I'm expected to eat this and, later, endure the aroma of bacon sizzling in the skillet."

There was a hint of amusement behind the accusing statement.

"That would be cruel, wouldn't it?" Sharon agreed with an impish look in her hazel eyes. Actually her menu plans for breakfast had consisted of dry cereal and toast, but she didn't enlighten him at this stage.

"You know it would," Ridge countered and picked up the spoon on his tray. It hovered just above the bowl of oatmeal while he cast another glance at her. "There are no knock out drops in here, are there?"

"None," she promised and lightly crossed her heart, making a playful gesture of taking an oath. She turned from the bed and started for the door with her coffee cup.

"Where are you going?" His question came quickly, light with surprise at her intention to leave.

Sharon half-turned to glance at him. "I'm going to my room to get dressed."

"You can do that later. Stay here and keep me company while I eat." The request was accompanied by a crooked, coaxing smile that was almost impossible to resist.

When he chose to exercise it, Ridge was a master at the fine art of persuasion, relying on his potent charm rather than male dominance to get his way. Sharon was by no means immune to that brand of appeal. She was conscious of wavering, an invisible force in those glittering blue eyes pulling her back to the bed.

The first step was taken before she even realized it. The discovery seemed to jolt her. Sharon quickly altered her course, angling away from the bed toward the dresser where a radio sat.

"It's just about time for the market reports," she said. "You can listen to the radio while you eat your breakfast." After she turned the radio on, she made sure it was tuned to the local Colorado station carrying the grain and livestock reports. The announcer's voice spilled from the speaker, and Sharon turned to glance over her shoulder at Ridge. "Is that loud enough?"

"Yeah, but it isn't much company." There was a degree of wryness in the slanting line of his mouth. "A radio just talks; it doesn't talk back."

"That should make you happy," Sharon replied dryly and headed again toward the hallway. "I'll be back to pick up the tray a little later."

114

# Chapter Seven

Numerous washings and wearings had faded the jeans Sharon wore until they were a color between pale blue and blue-white. Her blouse was a blue and gray madras plaid, its bleeding pattern seeming to match the jeans. A pair of tortoise-shell barrettes pinned the sides of her toffee-brown hair away from her face, and a pair of dun-colored cowboy boots with run-down heels clad her feet. It was the usual garb she wore around the family home, and Sharon didn't dress differently in Ridge's house.

On her way to the kitchen to fix a light breakfast for herself, she swung by his room to pick up the tray. The radio was twanging out a country song when she entered. Ridge was reclining on the pillows supporting his back, a bare, muscled arm curled behind his head. A half-smoked cigarette dangled from his mouth. Although the curling smoke screened his gaze, she felt his slowly scanning study.

"All finished?" Her airy question was an attempt to break the trace of tension she felt. Even before

Sharon reached for the tray, she had already noticed Ridge had eaten nearly every bit of his breakfast.

He lifted a hand to remove the cigarette from his mouth. "You can take it away." With a turn of his head, he made sure he tapped the cigarette into the ashtray on the bedside table. His glance ran sideways to continue its slightly narrowed inspection of her. "Those jeans don't do anything for you."

Sharon faltered at the unexpected, and uncomplimentary, remark. "Thanks a lot." There was no humor in her laughing retort.

His mouth lifted at the corners but didn't finish the movement in a smile. "If I hadn't seen you in that silk robe and nightgown, I wouldn't have known you had such a nice shape. It's a pity you didn't leave it on. It clung to your figure in all the right places."

She hadn't been aware he'd noticed, but very little escaped those keen blue eyes. "I could hardly run around all day in my night clothes," she declared with a scoffing laugh that was on the weak side.

"I wouldn't have objected in the least," Ridge murmured dryly.

"Well, I would," Sharon responded with a certain stiffness, a little unsettled by the physical interest he was expressing, and walked to the door with the tray of breakfast dishes. "I'm going to the kitchen and fix myself something to eat. Was there anything you needed before I do?"

There was a hesitation, as if Ridge considered a

possible answer and rejected it. "No," he said finally. "But you can bring me another cup of coffee after you've finished."

"Okay."

Taking Ridge at his word, Sharon ate her breakfast of corn flakes and toast, washed their combined dishes, then poured his second cup of coffee and took it to him. The disc jockey on the radio was giving the day's weather forecast when she entered the room.

"—highs in the upper 60s today. Looks like summer's just around the corner, folks," the drawling voice concluded.

"It's going to be a nice day," Sharon observed after darting a glance at the radio. "Here's your coffee."

"I was beginning to think you forgot." He shifted his position slightly and winced.

"I didn't." She set it on the table near the ashtray, conscious of his bare-chested form and the rusty darkness of his hair in her side vision.

When she turned to leave, Ridge inquired, "Where are you going now?" with a trace of exasperation in his voice.

She turned again to the bed, vaguely defensive. "I was going to make my bed and straighten up the house. Why?"

"When am I going to get my bath and a shave?" he asked, folding his arms across his middle, an action that exhibited both patience and challenge.

"What?" Sharon blinked at him.

"When are you going to give me my bath?"

Ridge repeated the question, a dancing light appearing in his blue eyes. Dumb struck for an instant, all Sharon could do was open her mouth. He mockingly chided her for wearing such a blank look. "All babies get a bath in the morning. I remember you telling me before breakfast that I was just an overgrown baby. So how about my bath?" When she continued to stare at him in disbelief, he reasoned, "If I were still in the hospital, a nurse would be giving me a bath."

"You can't be serious," Sharon managed to breathe out shakily.

"I'd do it myself if I wasn't so sore I can hardly stand to move," he replied, again in a reasonable tone that conflicted with the taunting gleam in his eyes. He rubbed a hand across the bristly growth of a night's beard. "I'd like to get cleaned up—and you're here to look after me."

It was extremely difficult to argue either with his logic or his request. As a matter of fact, Sharon couldn't find any legitimate excuse to refuse him, although she searched wildly for a plausible reason.

Heat began to rise in her face at the thought of washing him all over. Sharon turned away from the bed so that Ridge wouldn't see her reddening cheeks. If it was his intention to embarrass her, she didn't want to give him the satisfaction of knowing he had succeeded.

"I'll be back in a minute with a washbasin and some towels." She cast the statement over her shoulder in a remarkably level voice and headed quickly toward the private bath that adjoined his room.

The task of finding a washbasin and gathering washcloth, soap, and towels gave Sharon the necessary time to pull herself together. A degree of detachment was required and she struggled to achieve the necessary poise and quiet her jittery nerves.

Armed with a pair of thick bath towels, a basin full of soapy water, and a washcloth, Sharon emerged from the bathroom, appearing outwardly calm and, she hoped, professional. She ignored the faint smile that played around the corners of his mouth as she walked directly to the bed and placed the basin on the nightstand.

In her baby-sitting days, she'd had more than ample practice bathing toddlers and young tots. The trick was to pretend Ridge was the overgrown child she had claimed him to be.

"How do you want to go about this?" Ridge asked, not cooperating at all. "Do you want to begin at the bottom and work your way up? Or at the top and work your way down?"

It was a simple question, but the way her mind was working, she read something much more suggestive into it. And she suspected that Ridge had counted on that. Distance from those taunting blue eyes seemed preferable. Also, Sharon didn't think she'd find anything very sexy about his feet, so she opted for them as a beginning.

"The bottom."

Striving to keep that air of clinical detachment, she tossed aside the bedcovers to expose the lower half of his body and draped one of the bath towels across his hips. She could sense the laughter in his glance at that action, but she steadfastly kept her attention on what she was doing. She shook out the second towel and lifted the leg farthest from her, sliding the towel under it so the bedding wouldn't get wet.

When she turned to the basin to wet the washcloth and soap it up, she was conscious of Ridge's glinting look. Silently he lay there, giving every indication that he was enjoying all this immensely —at her expense.

The knowledge fed an inner irritation. Sharon was a bit more vigorous than was entirely necessary when she began scrubbing his leg and foot. His soap-slicked skin made her more aware of the rope-hard muscles in his calf and thigh. She concentrated on his foot.

"Be sure to get between my toes," Ridge instructed and wiggled them slightly to draw her attention to them.

After an instant's hesitation, Sharon complied. Her lips were clamped shut against the building tension inside. *He's just a little boy*, she kept telling herself, adding, *—with big feet.*

"When my mother gave me a bath, she always played 'This little pig went to market' with my toes." The thickness of dry amusement was in his voice.

His reference to himself as a small boy completely destroyed her pretense. By no stretch of the imagination could she kid herself into believing any longer that this wasn't a man's leg she was washing.

"This is ridiculous," Sharon muttered under her breath and wetted the cloth again so she could rinse the soap from his leg.

"Is something wrong?" Ridge asked in false innocence.

"Whatever gave you that idea?" Her answer was terse, with none of its implied amusement, as she rinsed the soap from his leg and dried it.

"I thought I heard you mutter something," he persisted dryly.

"Well, you must have been hearing things." She shifted the towel under his other leg and began washing it with an air of determined indifference to mask her heightened sensitivity.

She was conscious of his watching eyes and calmly folded arms. It increased her awareness of the amount of bare flesh exposed to her sight. Sharon wished she could pretend Ridge was a stranger. Maybe then she wouldn't be wondering what was going through his mind.

It was worse when she rubbed the washcloth over the top of his thigh and the smoothly muscled flank. Her heart racketed against her rib cage in disturbed reaction.

"I guess you don't want to play 'Piggy went to market,'" Ridge concluded when she had finished scrubbing his foot and moved back up his leg.

"No, I'm not going to play 'Piggy went to market.'" She stepped to the basin and rinsed out the washcloth. "But if a rubber ducky will keep you quiet, I'll see if I can find one."

He tipped his head back to look at her. "Am I bothering you?"

"Do birds fly?" Sharon retorted and briskly wiped the soap from his leg to dry it.

Ridge waited to reply, timing it for the moment when she began washing his outstretched arm. "What made you think about birds?"

Her hand paused along his flexed bicep as Sharon darted a glance at the lazy and inquiring expression on his face. In her mind there was an immediate word association of "birds" with "bees." It was hardly surprising. Since she was engaged in the intimate act of washing him, how could she not be aware of his sex—and her own? She began to feel very warm, and a growing agitation within started to affect the natural rhythm of her breathing.

"I really couldn't say why I did." Sharon attempted an indifferent shrug but answered truthfully.

To wash his other arm, she had to lean partially across him. The focus of his attention was on the nearness of her face rather than on what she was doing. As he lazily inspected her, he observed every nuance of her expression, adding to the havoc he was already creating in her senses. Her pulse was behaving erratically—slowing down, skipping beats, then taking off again.

"Having someone bathe you is a very enjoyable experience," Ridge commented idly.

"I'm glad someone's enjoying this." It was a low retort, close to being muttered. Sharon rubbed the soapy washcloth over the muscled ridges of his shoulders, under his throat, and across the top of his chest, taking care not to get the elastic bandage around his ribs wet.

"Aren't you?" A smiling knowledge lurked behind the blue surface of his eyes.

"I'm having a ball," she mocked. Rinsing out the washcloth, she went over the same territory again.

"I thought so," he murmured.

Sharon nearly blushed because it was true, despite all this self-consciousness. She was enjoying this excuse to touch nearly every part of him, not once but a total of at least three times, when she counted washing, rinsing, and drying. Through with the washcloth, she dropped it into the basin and picked up the towel to pat dry his damp skin.

"When I get up and around—" Ridge had to lift his chin high to avoid the bulky towel when she dried his throat and chest "—remind me to return the favor and give you a bath."

Sharon faltered but recovered quickly and straightened, all brisk and efficient. "I think I'd rather manage by myself."

"You don't know what you're missing," he warned.

"I guess that's my loss," she countered and dipped her hand into the basin for the washcloth again. "Do you want to wash your own face, or shall I do it for you?"

During a small hesitation, Ridge seemed to measure the glint in her hazel eyes. "I think I'd better do it myself," he decided. "You look like you might want to push that washcloth down my throat."

"Me?" Sharon returned innocently. "The thought never entered my mind." But she had been thinking about the hard contours of his face beneath her fingers, so it was just as well that he did the job himself. She soaped up the washcloth and handed it to him, then put the towel within easy reach. "I'll bring your razor and comb from the bathroom while you finish up." When she reached the doorway to the bathroom, she paused and turned to look over her shoulder. "Don't forget to wash behind your ears."

There was a sound of amusement, close to a laugh that didn't get finished, checked by painful rib and stomach muscles that wouldn't permit it without severe protest. Sharon swung on into the bathroom to collect the items.

Ridge had finished when she came back and crossed to the bed. Before she handed him the electric razor, she reached behind the bedstand and plugged the cord into the outlet, then passed the razor to him.

"Do you need a mirror?" she asked. "Or can you shave just by feel?"

"I can get by without a mirror," he said, rubbing a hand over the stubble on his jaw.

The hum of the razor filled the room as Sharon

gathered up the damp towels and the washbasin and carried them back to the bathroom. By the time she had hung the towels and washcloth up to dry, rinsed out the basin, put it away, and returned to the bedroom, Ridge had shaved and combed his mahogany dark hair.

"How do I look?" he queried.

As long as she ignored the bandaged ribs and bruised stomach, he looked vitally fresh, able to take on anything or anyone and win. But Sharon kept that opinion to herself.

"You look fine," she said and gathered the razor and comb from the table. "I'll just put these things away."

"You can bring me some clothes, too," Ridge instructed as she headed for the bathroom again.

"You don't need any," she retorted as she set the items on the bathroom sink counter and came back out. When she saw the argumentative look in his face, she reminded him of his promise. "You're going to stay in bed and rest, remember? Since you're spending the day in bed, there's no need to get dressed."

Grim and restless, he swung his gaze away from Sharon, flashing it around the room, then slicing it back to her as she approached the bed to reposition the sliding pillows supporting him.

"Dammit, I'll go crazy in here with nothing to do," he protested.

"You can listen to the radio and I'll bring some stock magazines for you to read." She punched the pillow into place behind him and straightened to leave.

"Where are you going?" His calloused fingers made a rough band around her wrist to detain her.

The warmth and strength of his hand seemed to flow into her veins. Sharon tried to react calmly to his hold, so that her pulse wouldn't leap against his thumb.

"I still haven't made my bed or straightened the house," she said. "And I need to find something to fix for your lunch."

"Stay here and keep me company," Ridge urged with a persuasive gleam in his lazy blue eyes.

When he was in this sexily cajoling mood, his male charm could be a potent thing. She felt its caressing tug on her emotions and shook her head in wary resistance.

"I'm here to take care of you, Ridge, not to keep you entertained," she countered smoothly, but his grip only tightened when she tried to pull her hand away.

The glint in his eye became more challenging and seductive, a kind of dare in its mocking depths. "I promised to stay in bed and rest, but only if you promised to stay with me." The pressure of his grip pulled her closer to the bed until she was awkwardly unbalanced, with her knees butting against the mattress while she leaned over it.

"You did no such thing," Sharon protested and tried to brace herself to keep from being pulled further by stretching her free hand on the mattress.

Ridge caught it, too, and held both wrists captive. It was too soon after bathing him to be this close. She'd barely had time to calm her hotly disturbed senses. Now the fresh scent of soap clinging to his bare skin was igniting them all over again.

"Sleeping alone is one thing," Ridge drawled. "But I'm not used to lying alone in a bed during the daytime. It isn't natural."

Needing leverage to combat the steady pull of his hands, Sharon put a knee on the mattress, but that left her with only one foot on the floor to act as an anchor. Before she could set herself to tug against his pulling hands, Ridge was dragging her across him.

"Be careful," she gasped, suddenly more worried about falling on his injured middle than she was about being hauled into the bed. "You're going to get hurt again."

"Not if you pay attention," he taunted and helped her climb over him to the wider side of the bed.

As soon as she was clear of him, she tumbled in an ungainly sprawl onto the mattress beside him. For several seconds, she lay there, vaguely irritated because she knew she hadn't struggled very hard to avoid this. It was no use pretending that she hadn't fought harder because she was afraid of hurting him. That was just a handy excuse.

The mattress moved under his shifting weight. Sharon turned her head to look at him warily, one wrist still shackled by his encircling grip. He had slid off the pillows and was now stretched alongside her, half turned, with his dark head supported by a bent arm. The glinting caress of his mocking blue eyes tightened her stomach.

"This is ridiculous." Her protest was hardly more than a husky murmur. "I have work to do."

"You're here at Latigo to take care of me, not to make beds or clean house." Ridge let go of her wrist, but she wasn't free of his touch as his hand moved to the side of her neck. His fingers were gentle and caressing while his thumb lightly stroked the curve of her throat. "Taking care of me is a full-time job."

A sweet tightness of tormenting misery welled in her throat at his comment, choking off her voice. It was a full-time job she wanted desperately—all over again. She hadn't learned a thing. Her adolescent crush had grown into love. It wasn't that Ridge had the power to disturb her so completely. It was the love she felt for him that gave him that power.

From experience, Sharon knew that Ridge didn't love women. He made love to them, but there was never any emotional commitment behind it. Knowing that, she had to guard against ruining her life over him a second time.

Bending his head he nuzzled her lips, reveling in their softness before settling firmly onto them. The slow and heady kiss dragged a response from inside her. She returned the slow, sensual movement of his mouth against hers. The sweet intensity of her pleasure bordered on pain, but she managed to suppress most of her longing.

Momentarily satisfied with the response to his first intimate foray, Ridge drew back to study her through half-closed eyes. Sharon tried to show no reaction as his fingertips explored her features, spending a lot of time around her mouth.

"Ridge, you're going to hurt yourself." Sharon attempted to reason with him. "You're supposed to rest and take it easy."

His mouth came back to make another claim on her lips, while her pulse skyrocketed at his seductive insinuation. Her hands moved tentatively to the top of his chest and the hard bones of his shoulder. Their contact with his flesh was limited by his injuries, as Sharon subconsciously avoided aggravating his soreness. His strongly stimulating kiss was skillfully drawing out her responsiveness, not letting her contain it.

The roaming caress of his hand had moved down to the back of her hip, gently applying pressure to urge her closer. In absent compliance, Sharon shifted nearer until she came up against the barrier of his long legs. She became conscious of a new assault as the solid outline of his muscular thighs became imprinted on her legs and the heat of his body burned through her clothes.

As his mouth followed a slow, wandering trail across her cheek to her ear, her self-control became undermined by the eroding force of her desire. His warm breath was a sexual stimulus to the sensitive opening of her ear, sending excited quivers over her skin. Sharon sunk her teeth into the soft inside of her lower lip, biting back the moan that rose in her throat.

His fingers pushed the collar of her blouse away from her neck as his warm lips moistly nuzzled the pulsing cord. She struggled to surface from this whirlpool of raw sensation when his hand continued down her blouse collar until it encountered the first button. She felt his fingers working to loosen it and brought her hand down on his wrist.

"You are really into children's games this morning, aren't you?" The pitch of her voice was husky and disturbed as she challenged him.

"Why?" He was distracted from his nuzzling study of her throat long enough to look at her, most of his interest centering on her lips.

"Isn't this a version of 'Button, button, who's got the button'?" she accused on a breathless note, her hand tightening on his wrist even as the first button was slipped free of its buttonhole.

His lip corners were tugged upward. "Ah, but it's the adult version," Ridge informed her with dryly mocking amusement, and bent his head again to her neck. His fingers were already moving on to the next button in line.

Sharon let go of his wrist and tried to get in the way of his hand. "Will you stop unbuttoning my blouse?" There was a tinge of desperation in the exasperated tone of her protest.

"I'd be happy to," he murmured against the throbbing pulse in her neck, "if you'll tell me some other way to get the thing off."

Her breathing became agitated and deep as she tried to interfere with his deftly working fingers. Suddenly, something in their actions reminded her of the handslap game she'd played as a child. The situation struck her funny and laughter bubbled in her throat, venting some of the sexual tension that had brought her nerves to a state of panic.

The laughter tumbled helplessly from her, turning her weak. Confused, Ridge lifted his head to gaze at her, the blue of his eyes reflecting some of the amusement that had her in its throes.

"What's so funny?" he asked.

"Doesn't this remind you of two kids playing that handslap game?" Suppressed and breathless laughter was in her voice as she sought to share her humor with him.

Giving in to the laughter had been a grave mistake, a fact Sharon discovered when she felt the warm sensation of his hand gliding under the material of her blouse and onto her ribcage below the underswell of her breast. While she was laughing, he had finished unbuttoning her blouse. There was nothing funny about the situation anymore. It was purely erotic, made even more so by the lusting desire in his lazy eyes.

"Damn you, Ridge Halliday." Her voice trembled in disturbed reaction. "You don't play fair."

"How the hell do you think I win all the time?" he taunted softly and leaned to bury her lips with the hard pressure of his kiss while his hand cupped itself to the taut underside of her breast.

She was lost in a mindless blur of sensation that

swept her deeper and deeper into his embrace. The smell of his skin and the hot taste of his tongue were aphrodisiacs to her senses. Her restless hands were fascinated with the hard sinew and bone of his naked shoulders, his flesh warm and vital to her touch, the elasticized band around his ribs always reminding her of his injuries.

Caught between conflicting needs, Sharon felt hopelessly torn. The instinct of self-preservation insisted she must stop this before it went any further, but his warm lips were already nuzzling the valley between her breasts, then mounting a slope to encircle its pointed peak. With deliberate thoroughness, Ridge was conquering her body one area at a time. The part of her that loved him was willing to concede the battle.

Slowly he began to backtrack to her throat and neck, his body shifting slightly away from her. At first, Sharon didn't understand his intention until her stomach muscles contracted under the touch of his hand as it moved to the waistband of her jeans. There was a wild fluttering in the pit of her stomach, raw longing rushing intensely through her.

"Ridge—" The sane half of her that wanted to protect her from future hurt attempted a protest.

"You're enjoying it, aren't you?" His teeth gently tugged at the lobe of her ear.

"Yes," she admitted with groaning reluctance.

"We can fool around like this all day," he murmured with suggestive promise.

It was a poor choice of words, but she was

ultimately glad he'd used them, because they swayed her out of her indecision. She rolled away from him, taking advantage of the soreness that didn't permit him to move swiftly, and swung off the bed. Sharon heard his muffled grunt of pain when he tried to follow her, but she didn't turn around as she hurriedly, though shakily, rebuttoned her blouse.

"What are you doing?" Ridge finally asked after he'd gotten his breath back from that shafting pain.

"I told you I have work to do," she stiffly reminded him.

He didn't accept that explanation. "Come back here and tell me what happened." The invitation was lazily offered.

"No." She could feel his eyes on her.

"Why?" he countered smoothly.

Swiveling at her hips, Sharon half-turned to meet his steady gaze. Hard determination burned cold in her hazel eyes, able to look at him impassively.

"Maybe I don't want to be the one who winds up being the fool when you're through fooling around," she stated in a hard, flat voice.

She saw the brief, upward flick of his eyebrow and the subsequent narrowing of his eyes as he reassessed her. At the moment she didn't care what lay behind those solid features or his silence. She left the room while she had the chance.

# Chapter Eight

It seemed she was going in and out of his room all day long. Everytime she turned around, Ridge was impatiently calling for her. Sometimes it was for something as trivial as emptying his ashtray, sometimes he wanted a cup of coffee or to complain that the radio was still too loud and keeping him from taking a nap. Naturally, an hour later he wanted the radio turned up.

Late in the afternoon, he relented and took a pain pill. Sharon was able to fix supper without any interruption from him. When she carried the tray into his room she caught him out of bed. Although Sharon couldn't say that she had gotten used to seeing him lying half-naked in the bed, partially covered with a sheet, it was certainly more unnerving to see his long, lean body out of the bed, clad only in a thin pair of soft cotton jockey shorts. Anger seemed the best way to cover up the effect he was having on her.

"What do you think you're doing?" she demanded as she watched him moving gingerly across the room to the bed. "I thought I told you to stay in bed. What are you doing out of it?"

"I had to use the bathroom. Somehow, I just didn't think you'd want to lend your assistance in that department," he shot back in faintly taunting sarcasm.

Sharon flushed darkly and continued into the room, averting her gaze while he managed to climb into bed on his own. "I could have helped you to the door and back," she insisted stiffly.

He had noticed the high points of color in her cheeks and smiled in satisfaction. "Your poise is slipping, nurse," he mocked. "Remember, you have a brother, so a man's anatomy isn't likely to embarrass you."

There was no response for that, but she tried. "Maybe I was more embarrassed by my imagination than by your body?" Sharon suggested coolly and set the tray on his lap. "Eat your supper."

When she started to turn away from the bed, his hand lightly touched her arm. "Sharon, I'm sorry." It was a low, rough apology, offered reluctantly, as usual. Ridge sighed heavily. "Hell, I'm bored and miserable—and I'm just taking it out on you because you happen to be on the spot." She could understand that even if it wasn't an adequate excuse. "Will you bring your food in here and eat with me?"

His drawling appeal for her company was very tempting. Against her better judgement, Sharon found herself agreeing.

It turned out to be a very companionable meal without a lot of conversation. Ridge seemed to be on his best behavior, not needling her with any of his bold remarks. It was as if they were back on a friendly footing, although Sharon knew it would take only one misstep for everything to go haywire.

While she was washing the dishes, her parents came by to see how Ridge was doing and whether there was anything Sharon needed. She had written out a short grocery list of soft foods to fix for Ridge, which she went over with her mother.

"While you're in town, would you buy him a pair of pajamas and a robe?" Sharon added. "He doesn't own any."

"His lack of proper attire is slightly indecent—or so your father thought," her mother laughed softly. "Of course, he thought that only because you're here taking care of Ridge."

"Sharon!!" Her name was shouted from the bedroom, the voice unmistakably belonging to Ridge.

"What?!!" she hollered back, then said to her mother in an aside, "I've learned to shout first. That way I don't have to walk back to get whatever it is that he wants."

"We need some coffee!!" came the answer.

"Coming!!" She reached for the coffeepot and glanced wryly at her mother. "I haven't decided whether he simply enjoys having me at his beck and call or if he's only trying to get back at me because I made him stay in bed all day."

"It's probably a combination," her mother replied wisely.

It was late in the evening before her parents left. Her father stayed in the bedroom and talked ranching with Ridge while Sharon and her mother sat in the kitchen. Naturally, she found herself hopping up about every fifteen minutes to fetch something for Ridge.

When she said goodbye to her parents at the door and watched them walk to their pickup truck, it left her with an odd feeling. It was as if this house was her home—where she lived with Ridge on a permanent basis. She closed the door and looked slowly around at the walls and ceilings with a sense of belonging.

"Stop dreaming, girl," she mentally gave herself a hard shake. She paused at Ridge's door long enough to tell him goodnight and then went on to bed.

As she lay awake in the melancholy darkness of her room, Sharon wished Ridge had been made differently. He was one of the Western breed, not exactly a rare type of man, because she'd met a few others who shared his characteristics. Cowboying and ranching were their life, and there wasn't any room for a wife and family. They enjoyed women and a wild time, but that was about the only role a female played in their lives.

Rolling over, she shut her eyes tightly and wondered why she had to fall in love with a man with lazy blue eyes who wouldn't settle down. It wasn't fair, not when she'd come so close to getting over him.

The second day was practically a repetition of the day before, except that Sharon suggested that Ridge do his own bathing and there wasn't any tussle in bed. Other than that, she insisted that he spend most of the day in bed, and Ridge found a hundred reasons to call her into the room, fetching and doing things for him. Her mother stopped by in the afternoon with the groceries Sharon had wanted, plus the pajamas and robe. Sharon delayed giving the latter two to Ridge until the next morning.

When Sharon carried in his breakfast tray, Ridge was ready to do battle. There was a hard gleam in his eye as she approached the bed. She was reminded of a range stallion, penned for the first time in his life.

"I'm not staying in bed today," he announced. "If I don't start moving around, I'll be so stove up I won't be able to move."

"I'm sure you're right," she said, taking him by surprise when she didn't argue with him.

While he was eating breakfast, Sharon went into her room and got the package containing the new pajamas and robe. She carried it into his bedroom and laid it on the sheet beside him.

"What's that?" Ridge glanced at her suspiciously.

"It's kind of a get-well present," she shrugged.

There was a smile in her hazel eyes as she watched him open it. The pajamas were on top, a deep blue cotton trimmed in a lighter, sky-blue shade. He held them up, chuckling in his throat, and slid her a sparkling blue glance.

"No doubt I'm expected to model these," he said, lifting out the matching robe.

"Indeed you are." She smiled back. "But that can wait until after you finish your breakfast."

"Tomorrow morning it's back to bacon and eggs," Ridge decreed as he looked at the bowl of cream of wheat with distaste.

"We'll see," was the only comment Sharon made before leaving him to eat the rest of his breakfast.

Later she came back for the tray. Since he didn't ask for any help dressing, Sharon didn't offer. She was in the kitchen, washing the breakfast dishes, when she heard his hesitant footsteps approaching. She turned as he reached the doorway and leaned heavily against the doorframe for support.

"Well? How do I look?" He lifted a hand in a modeling gesture to indicate his outfit.

But her first glance went to his rugged features, taking note of the haggard lines of suppressed pain. She could well imagine how very stiff and sore he was. Then she let her glance sweep over the blue robe covering the pajamas. The color seemed to intensify the brilliance of his blue eyes and the darkness of his coloring.

"You look terrific." She tossed out the compliment lightly, but it was true.

"I feel like some damned actor," he declared in a tone of self-disgust. "But at least if someone comes, I don't have to dive under the covers." He sighed heavily and looked at her. "I'll be happier when I can put on a pair of boots and jeans again."

"I know." She turned back to the sink, aware that when that day came, there would no longer be a need for her to take care of him.

There was a long pause, then Ridge asked, "What are you going to do this morning?"

"I thought I'd do some baking. Why?" She had all the ingredients to make a butterscotch pie, which had always been a favorite of Ridge's when he'd eaten at their house.

"No reason." He hesitated, then very grudgingly asked, "Would you help me into the other room? I'm not as mobile as I thought."

She quickly dried her hands on a towel and went over to his side. Grimly he put an arm around her shoulders and used her body for extra support. Every step seemed to jar him as she helped him into the living room. Her side glance caught the twinges of pain that managed to break through his severely controlled expression.

"Do you want to lie down and rest for awhile?" Sharon could tell that even this small amount of exertion had tired him.

"No." He rejected the idea out of hand. "Take me to the desk. I seem to have only enough strength to sit, so I might as well do all that paperwork that's been piling up." There was anger and self-disgust in his voice.

"Maybe it would help if you took a pill?" she suggested as she led him to the large desk.

"No. I want to make it through the day without any . . . if I can," he added the reluctant admission that maybe he couldn't endure as much as he thought.

Before the morning was over, Sharon discovered that just because Ridge was out of bed, it didn't lessen the number of his demands on her. His short temper quickly made it clear that he resented needing her help as much as he resented his own inability to take care of himself.

When she looked back on the morning, she could remember Ridge saying only one nice thing and that had been at lunchtime after he'd eaten his second slice of pie. "That's better than your mother's," he'd said.

After an hour of paperwork in the afternoon, Ridge finally admitted to being tired and lay down on the sofa to rest. He refused to go into the bedroom. Sharon put a casserole in the oven for supper and moved quietly into the living room to find him sleeping soundly, a frown creasing his face.

The house was quiet and very still. She could feel the tension in her shoulders and neck. Between suppressing her natural feelings for Ridge and the incessant demands he'd made on her in the last four days, it had been hectic. Not once had there been any break.

Her gaze strayed to the window, where the sunshine of a Colorado afternoon blazed in. There was no better opportunity to take a walk than now, while Ridge was sleeping. Stealthily, she slipped out the front door.

Outside, Sharon wandered away from the house and its ranch buildings. A wind swept over the rugged tableland and lifted her toffee-colored hair to rush its fingers through it. She turned a far-seeing gaze to the land around. It was a wild stretch of country, caught between the rugged canyon-lands to the north where Butch Cassidy and his gang had once roamed and the raw, spectacular mountains of the Colorado Rockies to the south and east.

It was a land of cattle and sheep ranches and not much else except perhaps its untold fortune in oil shale. The Piceance Basin and the Book Cliff Mountains were her home. She pulled her gaze in, studying the Latigo range. The ranch showed the care and pride of its owner. Its fences were strong and well built; its buildings were painted and in good repair; and its livestock were sleek and well fed.

Wildflowers were sprinkled along the fenceline, as many-colored as a painter's palette. The minute she saw them, Sharon knew they were just what the house needed to give it some life. She picked a big bunch so that she could make several bouquets.

She was humming to herself when she entered the house by the back door with her armload of flowers. She nudged the door shut with her hip and started for the sink.

"Where the hell have you been?" Ridge demanded, lurching into the doorway. "I've been through this whole damn house looking for you, calling until I'm damned near hoarse!"

"You were sleeping, so I went for a short walk. I haven't been gone that long," Sharon replied with a confirming glance at the wall clock.

She wasn't about to apologize for taking a walk. She felt she had earned that much. She began opening cupboard doors until she found the shelf where she'd seen the flower vases.

"Why didn't you tell me where you were going?" Ridge demanded as he crossed to the sink.

"I would have had to wake you up to do that, and I didn't think that would make you very happy," Sharon explained with a calmly unmoved glance at him.

"You're supposed to be taking care of me—not out somewhere walking," he muttered in a disgruntled tone. "When I woke up and realized you weren't here, I didn't know what to think." He ran a hand through his hair, rumpling it more than it already was.

"Don't tell me that you actually missed me?" She ran a wondering eye over him as she filled the vases with water.

His gaze at her became steady. A hint of a smile began to break through his angry expression. "Yes, I missed you."

A little thrill of gladness went through her, despite her attempts not to let his admission mean too much. She busied her hands with the wildflowers, arranging a bunch of them in a vase.

"The next time you decide to go for a walk while I'm sleeping," Ridge said as he hooked a hand around her waist, pulling her sideways so that she stood closer to him, "I want you to either wake me up and tell me where you're going or leave a note pinned to my chest."

His gaze was lightly mocking as he made his request. Sharon pushed at his hand, trying to shove it off her hipbone. She was all too conscious of her shoulder resting against his chest and the nearness of his mouth.

"Ridge, will you behave yourself?" she demanded patiently while she tried to check the rush of her pulse.

"Not until you promise me." His finger caught the point of her chin and turned it so that she faced him.

The smoky blue of his eyes held her gaze, absorbing her completely. "I promise." She could hear the huskiness in her voice.

Bending his head, he rubbed his mouth over the outline of her lips, tantalizing her until she could barely breathe. The man smell of him filled her senses as her faint breath mingled with the warm force of his.

"Damn, but you have the softest lips," he said against them.

"Damn, but you swear a lot," she murmured, wishing he would stop talking and kiss her.

Instead, he pulled his head back at her reply. "Does it bother you?" There was a concerned look on his face.

She found his question curious and tested it. "Why? Would you stop it if I did?"

His mouth quirked wryly. "Probably not, but I'd watch my language a little more closely around you."

"Well, it doesn't bother me," Sharon assured him and turned back to her bouquet, but his willingness to make the attempt indicated a respect for her. She liked that. But she held that knowledge close inside her, not letting him see how much a little thing like that meant to her.

The back door opened and Ridge released her, shifting his position to create a space between them as Scott walked into the kitchen.

"You're finally up and about," her brother observed. "How are you feeling?"

"Better," Ridge nodded affirmatively and levered himself away from the sink counter.

Out of the corner of her eye, Sharon noticed the way he disguised the difficulty he had walking as he moved toward the table and chairs in the kitchen. He didn't want Scott to see just how much trouble it was for him.

"Sit down." He motioned her brother to a chair. "We'll have some coffee. Sharon, pour us a cup."

It was on the tip of her tongue to point out that he'd been standing beside the coffee pot and could just as easily have poured himself a cup and carried it to the table, but she held back the words. Instead, she took two cups from the shelf, filled them with coffee, and carried them to the table for Ridge and her brother. Scott glanced at her as if he expected her to join them, but Sharon went back to the sink and began arranging the wildflowers in the vases.

As she listened to the hum of their voices, the moment seemed part of a familiar pattern. She'd lost count of the number of times she'd been a party to their conversations over the years. If there had been any change, it was simply that she had stopped blindly adoring Ridge. She loved him, but not blindly—futilely, probably, but not blindly.

Satisfied with the riot of blossom and color in the three vases, Sharon carried two of them into the living room, setting them in strategic places to liven the room. The third, a small vase, she set at the back of the kitchen table where it would be out of the way when they sat down to a meal. Then she stepped back to study the effect critically.

"How does it look?" she asked absently of the two men at the table. Her brother had an eye for such things as background color and proportionate sizes of objects in their settings.

"That's fine," replied Scott, never one to elaborate when something was right.

"Look what happens when you let a woman into your house for a few days," Ridge mocked, sliding Sharon a dryly amused glance. "All of a sudden, she starts setting flowers all over the place. I'm surprised she hasn't rearranged the furniture."

"I've been thinking about it," she retorted, vaguely irritated by his chiding comment.

"Well, don't," he smiled slowly. "I like things the way they are."

It only confirmed what she already knew. He was satisfied with his home and his life the way it was, minus a woman's touch.

"I can believe that." Her voice was flat and cool as Sharon broke the pattern and didn't stay in the kitchen to listen to them talk. She went into another part of the house and searched for something to do.

Before Scott left, he went to look for her to see if there was anything she needed. Ridge stood in the background, watching her with a keenly assessing eye. It was slightly unnerving to have him taking her apart and examining each piece.

"Why don't you stay for supper, Scott?" Sharon invited, suddenly wanting her brother's presence to shield her from Ridge. It was one thing knowing that he didn't need her in his life, but it was another to hear him say it.

"I can't tonight," her brother refused. "I promised Soames I'd be over to his place tonight and take a look at that round baler he wants to sell."

"It's just as well." Ridge tried to hide his hobbling gait as he moved closer to include himself in the conversation. "You wouldn't like the food. You should see what your sister's been feeding me."

"Come over tomorrow night," Sharon issued a second invitation to her brother, ignoring Ridge's mocking complaint about his diet of soft foods. "Ridge should be able to handle a *real* meal by then. I'll fix some roast beef and you can help him celebrate."

"I'll come," Scott accepted.

While Ridge had a last word with her brother, Sharon excused herself and returned to the kitchen to check on the casserole in the oven. It was bubbling away, so she turned the oven temperature to its lowest setting and started fixing the side dishes she intended to serve with it.

After Scott left the house, Ridge hobbled into the kitchen, keeping a hand on the wall for support. Sharon barely glanced up when he entered, then swung away to remove the dirty cups from the table.

"You might as well sit down. Supper will be ready in a few minutes," she informed him in a brisk voice.

As she carried the cups to the sink, she heard the scrape of a chair leg on the tile floor. She picked up the damp dishcloth and walked back to the table to wipe its top. Ridge was standing behind the chair he'd pulled out, leaning both hands on it to rest before exerting his sore stomach muscles to sit down.

The small vase of wildflowers on the table seemed to taunt her with their presence—as unwanted as she was. As soon as she had finished wiping the table, Sharon picked up the vase. When she swung away from the table to carry the vase to the counter, Ridge's hand snared the crook of her arm.

"You can leave the vase on the table. It won't be in the way," he said.

She raised a cool glance to his face. "I thought

you didn't like flowers sitting around," Sharon challenged.

"After being cooped up in the house all this time, it's nice to see a bit of the outdoors," Ridge replied with a vague shrug and released her arm to touch one of the red blossoms with his finger. "They won't last long. In a few days, they'll be dead."

"I know." Abruptly, Sharon set the vase on the table and turned away, smoothing her hands down the front of her jeans as she walked to the stove, fighting a sick, clammy feeling.

The flowers wouldn't be in the house for long and neither would she. When she was gone, Ridge wouldn't miss her any more than he would miss the flowers. Quickly she began dishing the food into serving bowls before realizing she hadn't set the table.

All through the meal, Sharon was conscious of the hooded study of his gaze. When they had finished eating, she poured them each a cup of freshly brewed coffee and began clearing the dirty dishes from the table while hers cooled.

"I wasn't completely honest with you the other day when we had that heated discussion," Ridge said, breaking the silence that followed the meal.

"Which one?" Sharon asked smoothly, because there had been several discussions that might be described as heated, and continued covering the bowls of leftovers and stowing them in the refrigerator.

"That day at the creek, before I got stomped on by that bull," he replied.

For an instant, his answer made her pause in midmotion, then she went back to her task more vigorously than before. She remembered the conversation much too vividly—and the bitter hurt and wounded pride that had ensued.

"I think just about everything was said that day," she said curtly and walked to the sink, conscious of his watchful eyes.

"Not quite everything," Ridge paused. "Would you come over and sit down? It's difficult to talk to somebody when they keep darting all over the room."

"I can hear you just fine. I don't have to sit down to listen," Sharon countered and began running water in the sink so she could put the dirty dishes in to soak.

"Your coffee is getting cold."

"I'll warm it up when I'm through here," she stated.

A heavy sigh came from him. Then his chair was pushed back from the table and she tensed at his unsteady approach. She squirted detergent into the water filling the sink and began setting the supper dishes into it. She felt the touch of his hands on her shoulders, stilling her movements.

"You accused me of giving you encouragement when you had that schoolgirl crush on me, and I admitted that I did." His voice was low, the vibration of it seeming to come through his hands to go inside her. "What I didn't tell you was that I found you to be a very tempting morsel. The problem came when I realized I wanted to do a lot more than just kiss you—and I knew you were so crazy about me that you'd let me."

Her cheeks grew hot. His hands started to move down her arms, their action too close to a caress. Sharon grabbed the dishcloth and began scrubbing at the dishes in the sink, forcing his hands off her arms, but they settled on her waist.

"I'm not even sure about that," she said tensely, denying she had been so besotted with him back then that she would have gone all the way. "If that's what you believed, what stopped you?" she challenged bitterly, not wanting this conversation to continue any more than she'd wanted the last. "Don't tell me your conscience wouldn't let you?"

"It wasn't my conscience as much as it was your brother," he stated.

"My brother?" Sharon frowned in confusion, her body poised motionless at his response.

"Scott was my best friend, practically a brother. You don't mess around with a guy's kid sister and expect him to stay your friend," Ridge explained. "That's why I kept 'hands off.'"

"What's the point in telling me this now?" Her lips came together in a grim line as she began washing the same plate over. "Is it supposed to make a difference?"

"The situation has changed." His hands began to move to the front of her waist, sliding across her stomach and causing her muscles to contract automatically at his touch.

"How?" She tried to breathe normally as she sliced a look backward out of the corner of her eye, feeling his breath stirring her hair.

"Because you've grown up." His crossing hands had drawn her against the full length of his body—her shoulders touching the solidness of his chest, her hips feeling the rub of his thighs. "Big brother is no longer under any obligation to protect you. You haven't done a bad job of taking care of me, so you must be able to take care of yourself."

"So?" Sharon didn't trust herself to say more than one word, afraid the thick disturbance within her would creep into her voice.

"So—while the situation has changed, I think other things haven't. Namely—that still I think you're a tempting morsel and I still want to do more than kiss you—and you want me to do more than that, too." His head dipped to graze his mouth along the curve of her neck.

Just for a second, Sharon let her lashes drift shut at the sheer sensuality of his caressing touch. Shuddering, she recognized that what Ridge had said was true. Knowing it also drove her out of his arms and spun her around to face him in a trembling fury.

"I think I hate all you maverick cowboys." Her voice was low and taut, riddled with bitter hurt. "Give you a good roping horse, some cattle, and a good time on Saturday night and that's all you need! Well, the rest of us want more than that! Some day I want a ring, a marriage license, and some children—in that order! You don't need those things—and what's worse, you don't want them!"

The beginnings of a glowering frown appeared on his face, narrowing his eyes to blue slits of color. Her hands were doubled into rigid fists as Sharon glared at him, fighting back the tears stinging her eyes.

"You turn me on, Ridge. I won't deny that," she declared. "But you were right when you said I could take care of myself. So from now on, you can just leave me alone!"

Hot tears were on the verge of spilling from her lashes. With long, angry strides, Sharon swept out of the kitchen. She had meant everything she'd said, and she didn't want to weaken her statement by breaking into tears. She didn't stop until she had reached her bedroom and shut the door, leaning weakly against it while silent sobs shuddered through her body.

It wasn't long until she heard the sound of Ridge moving along the wall outside her room. She stepped away from the door and impatiently wiped at the tears on her cheeks, breathing deeply to stop them. He knocked at her door.

"Sharon?" When she didn't answer, he knocked again, louder. "Sharon." He became more demanding. "Sharon, answer me!" She pressed her lips more tightly together. "Dammit, Sharon," he swore a warning.

"What?" The response was whipped out of her, but it angered her that he could prod her into speaking when she had vowed not to say a word.

There was a long silence before he spoke again, his tone considerably subdued and terse. "Don't bother with the dishes. I'll do them tonight."

She looked at the ceiling, wanting to laugh, but it hurt too much. He didn't even need her to wash the dishes! After a few seconds, she heard him moving away from her door.

# Chapter Nine

The next morning they didn't have much to say to each other, although his lidded blue gaze strayed to her often. Sharon was in the kitchen washing up the lunch dishes when she heard the heavy tread of cowboy boots.

When she turned, Ridge appeared in the doorway, dressed in snug-fitting jeans and a chambray shirt with a brown, work-stained cowboy hat shading his face. His rugged vitality and masculine roughness seemed to grip her by the throat.

"I'm going with Hobbs this afternoon and look over the ranch," he announced. "We're taking the truck."

It was on her tongue to ask if he felt up to it, but she doubted Ridge would admit that he wasn't. The same ridiculous male pride that had insisted on discharging himself from the hospital was now driving him to climb back into the seat of authority—even if it killed him.

"All right." Sharon swung back to the sink, tight-lipped in her disapproval.

She listened to his footsteps as he moved gingerly to the back door, knowing that as soon as he was with his foreman, Ridge would be gritting his teeth and walking as if he didn't hurt at all. Men, she thought with angry exasperation as she heard the door shut.

The dishes were done and she was putting the roast in the oven to slow-cook it to a tender doneness when the telephone rang. Sharon crossed the room to pick up the wall phone.

"Hello, Sharon?"

"Andy!" She recognized his voice with surprise. "I didn't expect you to call."

"You said to call on Saturday. Did you forget we have a date tonight?" Behind the joking tone there was a suggestion of hurt.

"No, I didn't forget." It had just slipped her mind. "I guess I didn't realize it was Saturday already."

"You're still staying at Latigo, I take it," he said, stating the obvious. "Isn't Halliday up and around yet?"

"He's up, but I think there's a difference of opinion about how well he's getting around," she murmured dryly.

"Is our date still on for tonight?"

Sharon hesitated only for a second. "Of course." After last night, the timing of this date couldn't have been better if she had planned it. Besides, Andy had always been able to boost her spirits, and they certainly needed boosting now.

"I'll pick you up between five-thirty and six."

* * *

Since her mother had sent over only every-day-type clothes, Sharon put on the peach-colored dress she'd worn the day she'd brought Ridge home from the hospital. Her light caramel hair was freshly shampooed and curled loosely on her shoulders. It was ego building to see her reflection in the oven door's glass window, even though she had a towel tied over the front of the full skirt to protect it.

The roast and its accompanying vegetables were done; there was a salad in the refrigerator, and some peas were in a pan on the stove burner ready to be warmed. The evening meal was virtually ready, except for the last-minute dishing up.

She turned around and skimmed the table with a glance, then realized there wasn't any bread out. Scott could eat half a loaf at one sitting. As she walked to the cupboard bread drawer to correct that oversight, she heard the back door open. A wave of tension tightened her nerves. When she turned back to the table with the loaf of bread in her hands, she was mentally prepared to meet Ridge.

Stiff legged and holding himself carefully, he entered the kitchen and more or less fell into a chair. He swept off his hat and dropped it on the table, then slumped against the chair back. There was an ashen quality about his face and the dullness of pain in his eyes. He was breathing in a slow, halting rhythm.

Without a word, Sharon left the bread on the table and went back to the cupboards, fetching him a glass of water and a pain pill. She set them in front of him. "Here you go, tough guy," she said unsympathetically. Ridge glanced at the pill and threw her a look, then tossed the pill into his mouth and washed it down with the water. "I probably wasted my time cooking this supper for you." Sharon declared, irritated with him for aggravating his condition. "Your stomach is liable to revolt at the first bite of roast beef."

"I'd forgotten I was going to get something to eat tonight for a change." The sharp edge in his voice was attributable to the pain he was obviously feeling. "How come Scott isn't coming to dinner?"

"As far as I know, he is." Sharon gave him a blank look.

"Then how come the table is only set for two people?" Ridge gestured to the two place settings, then his gaze swept over her, taking in the full-skirted dress. "And how come you're wearing that?"

"I'm going out tonight. I have a date with Andy Rivers," she announced into a room that suddenly seemed deadly quiet. "He should be here any time to pick me up."

"And what happens to me while you're out with your oil man?" It was a half-snarling demand. "You're supposed to be here to take care of me. That was the deal."

"I'm sure you'll manage to survive," Sharon murmured dryly. "Or you can ask Scott to stay and hold your hand if you're afraid of being alone for a few hours." Ridge lapsed into a thick silence that prickled her nerve ends. "Everything is ready for dinner. All you and Scott have to do is warm the peas and slice the meat."

There was no response. From outside came the slam of car doors. Sharon looked out the window to see her brother and Andy coming up the walk together after arriving separately. After a short glance at Ridge, she untied her apron and went to the door to greet them. He remained seated in the kitchen chair, all his attention centered on the cigarette he'd just lit.

The tension became electric after Sharon invited Andy into the house to wait while she got her jacket and purse. Ridge didn't say five words to him. She was seething at his rudeness when she walked out the back door with Andy.

"I'm sorry Ridge wasn't very polite to you, Andy." She felt she had to apologize for him. "He isn't in the best of moods right now."

"I'm used to it," he shrugged to show it hadn't bothered him. "There's a lot of ranchers that see red when they meet some guy who's interested in the oil shale that might be under their rangeland."

It seemed wisest to let Andy think along those lines. There was no reason to enlighten him about the circumstances that had preceded his arrival at the ranch. Tonight she had every intention of putting Ridge out of her mind.

Andy was fun, undemanding company. Even if she wasn't able to forget Ridge, Sharon did find herself relaxing and enjoying the outing. They made a long evening of it, driving all the way to

Glenwood Springs to take in a show and eat afterwards.

It was well after midnight when he drove to the end of the long lane into the headquarters of Latigo Ranch and stopped in front of the house. All the ranch buildings were dark, but lights burned in the house windows.

"It looks like somebody's waiting up for you," Andy observed as he switched off the engine.

"Ridge probably just left the lights on for me," Sharon reasoned, certain that after the strain of the afternoon, Ridge wouldn't have the stamina to stay up this late.

Andy climbed out of the car and came around to open her door. His hands rested companionably on her shoulders as they walked to the house, both fairly well talked out after the long drive.

"I enjoyed myself tonight," Andy said, then slid her a boyish grin. "I guess I always say that when I take you home, but it's true just the same. I guess it's because I feel I never have to prove anything to you—or come on like some heavyweight lover, which I'm not. I can just be myself."

"Me too." Sharon agreed with all he said, from her point of view as well.

"Some guy's gonna marry you one of these times and I'm gonna come back here and find out I've lost a friend," he declared with a mock shake of his head, stopping as they reached the door.

"We'll always be friends, Andy," she insisted.

"Not if you marry one of these 'cattle-or-die'

ranchers." With a nod of his head, he indicated the occupant of the house where they were standing.

It wasn't necessary to reply as Andy bent his head to kiss her goodnight. The outside light suddenly flashed on, its brightness blinding both of them and startling them into moving apart. The door opened and Ridge loomed in its frame, glowering at the pair of them.

"It's you," he muttered harshly and Sharon wondered who else he expected it to be. "I thought I heard a car door."

"You did." Sharon said, resentment starting to build at the way he continued to stand there, holding the door open.

"Are you coming in or not?" Ridge snapped impatiently.

She was ready to defy him, but Andy took the opportunity away from her. "Good night, Sharon. I'll give you a call when I'm going to be in the area again." There was almost a smile on his face as he bent his head and discreetly kissed her cheek.

"Good night, Andy," she returned and tossed a glaring look at Ridge.

Stubbornly, she waited outside a few minutes and watched Andy walk back to his car while Ridge impatiently cooled his heels at the door. Then, and only then, did she enter the house, her chin held at a coolly defiant angle.

The door was barely shut when Ridge pounced on her with an angry demand, "Do you know what time it is?"

"It must be after midnight," Sharon replied nonchalantly and swept into the living room. "How come you're still up? I thought you would have been in bed ages ago."

"I always stay up this late," he taunted her with the lie the way she had taunted him with her question. "I've been waiting up for you! What the hell do you think I'm doing up at this hour?!"

"That's what I thought." She turned on him, no longer trying to contain her anger.

"Just where the hell have you been?" Ridge demanded.

"That's none of your business!"

"It is my business!" he snapped. "You're staying in my house, so that makes me responsible for what happens to you."

"That's ridiculous," she declared scornfully. "Where I go and what I do are none of your affair."

"In case you don't know it, your brother doesn't think much of your oil man—and neither do I." He towered in front of her, bristling with anger.

"I don't care what you or Scott thinks of him. All that matters is what I think about Andy." She pointed at herself for emphasis. "I date whom I please—and stay out as late as I please. No one, not even my parents, tells me what to do—and you're certainly not going to."

"I suppose you think your oil man is going to give you a ring and a marriage license and those kids you said you wanted last night," Ridge jeered.

"He could," Sharon countered, angrily baiting him.

"Well, you can just forget him because you're not going out with him anymore," he informed her coldly, a muscle jumping in his jaw.

"Why? Because you say so?" she mocked him sarcastically, then hurled, "You don't own me, Ridge Halliday!"

"Do you wanna bet?" The taunting words were ground through his teeth as he roughly pulled her into his arms. She fought him wildly, pushing and struggling against the steel band that pinned her to his chest. By twisting her head, she managed to elude the mouth moving hotly over her face, but it was only temporary. "You're going to lose," Ridge said against her throat, his breath coming roughly. "And you know it."

Her own breath was coming in taut little sighing gasps as her pulse careened wildly out of control. It wasn't his strength she was fighting. It was the sensation of his lean, muscular length, the smell of his skin, and the husky sound of his voice that she fought to resist.

"I hate you," she said through her teeth, because he knew what he did to her when he touched her and he was taking advantage of it.

His mouth reached the corner of her lips. Of their own accord, they turned to seek his bruising kiss. Her fingers slowly uncurled from the balled fists she'd made of them and spread across his shoulders to dig fiercely into his shirt and the hard flesh under it. For long, hot moments, their lips mated in an angry union until it spawned passion.

She strained against him, arching her spine to shape herself more closely to the hard angles and planes of his body. Blood rushed through her veins, fevering her skin already heated from the restless, pressing movements of his hands, alternately caressing and molding her body to his needs.

When Ridge pulled his mouth from hers and came up for air, dragging in heavy, labored breaths, Sharon pressed her hot face against his chest. She could hear his heart pounding, loud and fast, competing with her own drumming pulse. His hand moved over the silkiness of her tawny hair to the side of her face and lifted it away from his chest. She tipped her head back to gaze up at him, seeing the smouldering satisfaction in his half-closed eyes. Ridge stroked his hand over her neck and throat, caressing its curving length. There was a faint tremor in his touch, betraying how disturbed he was.

"I'll never understand—" his husky voice was lower than a murmur and deep with desire "—how one person could have such incredibly soft lips and soft curves and still be so hardheaded and hard-nosed. Tell me now," he insisted, "where were you and that oil guy all this time?"

"We went to a show in Glenwood Springs, then ate afterwards," she whispered, her body aching for the thrust of his hips.

"He didn't make love to you?" His fingers

tightened ever so slightly on her neck, briefly applying pressure.

"No." Sharon turned her head in a negative movement. "Andy's a . . . friend."

"Why didn't you explain that to start with?" Ridge demanded gruffly. "Why did you put me through all this hell, wondering where you were and what you were doing with him? It kept getting later and later and I . . ." The rest was lost in a smothered groan as he punished her lips for the torment he'd been through, kissing them roughly and thoroughly, then drawing away. His hand tugged the elastic neckline of her dress off one shoulder to allow him to nibble on the sensitive bone, sending shivers of delight over her skin that raised her flesh.

"Were you jealous?" Sharon was dazed by the idea.

"Of him?" The look of amused scorn on his face when Ridge glanced at her, laughed away that fragile wisp of hope.

Crestfallen, Sharon lowered her gaze to the darkly tanned column of his throat. It had been a foolish thing to think, but just for a little while, she'd wondered. Then his warm lips were on her cheek, running over it in stimulating circles, and she closed her eyes to enjoy the heady bliss his touch created.

"Sharon," he murmured, tormenting her lips with the closeness of his mouth. "Let's stop fooling around and make love." His hands moved restlessly over her body, teasing her hips and breasts with his fleeting touch. "It's what we both want."

Although his statement wasn't a question, Sharon answered it like one. "Yes."

While her whole being seemed to clamor under the sweeping urgency of his kiss, some tiny fragment of her mind forced a recall of the words that had been said between them. It started an icy stream of thoughts that eventually chilled her ardor. As much as she loved Ridge and wanted him, she couldn't tolerate being a one-night stand in his life—and nothing he'd said had indicated he was offering her more than that.

She pushed with her hands to break free of him, inadvertently doing it against his cracked and broken ribs. His strangled cry of pain as he doubled over made Sharon realize what she'd done, but she felt little remorse. Considering how much he'd hurt her emotionally, he deserved to feel some pain of his own even if it was physical.

"What the hell are you trying to do?" he gasped and looked up at her with a frowning scowl. "They were just starting to heal and you damned near broke them all over again."

"You hypocrite!" She hurled the accusation at him.

"What are you talking about?" He straightened slowly and carefully, holding his rib cage and continuing to frown.

"You, pretending to be so righteous and upset because I was out so late with Andy Rivers!" Her scornful gaze raked him with disgust. "Trying to claim that you felt responsible for my reputation because I'm staying in your house. It was all lies! And I nearly believed your forked tongue. You come on 'holier than thou,' like Big Brother, and not ten minutes later, you're trying to proposition me into your bed!"

"It isn't like that, Sharon," he denied roughly.

"Oh, no?" she scoffed. "I told you last night and I'll tell you again. I'm not interested in what you have to offer, Ridge! I'm greedy. I want more than you can give me."

As she started to leave the room, Ridge tried to take a quick step to stop her and flinched at some inner shaft of pain. "Sharon." His hard voice called after her. "The last time you accused me of encouraging you. If I stepped out of line tonight, it was after I got encouragement from you."

"Then that makes us even, doesn't it?" She stopped long enough to throw the words at him.

For an instant, Sharon was held there by the sight of him, a lone figure in the middle of the room. His feet were planted slightly apart and his long arms were hanging loosely at his sides. His head was up and level. Nothing could be read in his features, ruggedly drawn in impassive lines. But it was the unstated things Sharon saw—the absolute self-reliance and the proud strength.

"Yes, we're even," Ridge acknowledged in a voice that rang flat and hard.

Turning, Sharon entered the hallway and walked past his room to her own. With unnatural calmness, she undressed and hung her dress up properly. It was as if she was trying to be as controlled and unaffected by events as Ridge appeared to be.

But when the lights were off and she was alone in the dark, it didn't seem so important anymore. Lying in bed, she slowly began to shake with sobs. As they grew stronger, she turned into her pillow and tried to muffle the sound in the feathery mass. It muted her crying and sopped up the tears running from her eyes.

A radio was turned on in the next room—Ridge's bedroom. The strains of a melancholy country song took up the silence. With it playing, Sharon didn't have to worry about Ridge hearing her, so she stopped holding back the violent ache that wrung her heart.

She finally cried herself into an emotionally exhausted sleep with the radio still playing its music in the background.

The next morning, Sharon drenched her puffy eyelids in cold water until her skin felt taut and frozen. She didn't take any pains with her appearance, skinning her hair away from her face and twisting a rubber band around its toasted-gold length. Her jeans were an old pair with patches on the seat, and her blouse was plain white cotton with a buttoned-down collar and long sleeves that she had rolled back at the cuff. Its whiteness, so close to her face, only emphasized her colorless, frozen complexion.

Her suitcase lay open on the bed, her underclothes lining the bottom of it. Gathering her few clothes on hangers in the closet, Sharon carried them to the bed and laid them beside the suitcase to begin folding them. As she slipped a blouse off its wire frame, she heard footsteps approach the door to her bedroom.

Since rising, she had ventured no further than the bathroom. No sound had come from the adjacent bedroom, so she had presumed that Ridge was still asleep—until she heard the footsteps. When she first awoke, the clock had shown the time as barely six in the morning. Evidently Ridge had been up before that.

The doorknob turned and the latch clicked in release. Her hands faltered slightly, then continued folding the blouse with steady precision. She didn't look at the door when it swung open, although her raw nerves were tensely aware of Ridge standing in the opening.

"I thought I heard you moving around in here," he said.

She laid the folded garment in the suitcase and reached for the next blouse, flicking a brief glance in his direction. But that swift look took in everything about him from the jeans and work shirt he wore to the impassive mask blanking out all expression from his male features except for the lazy sharpness of his blue eyes.

"If you want breakfast, you can fix it yourself," she informed him, her voice flat and emotionless.

"You're leaving," Ridge stated.

"Brilliant deduction." But her voice was too dry to put any sting in it.

"I thought you'd stay a couple more days." He sounded calm as he moved into the room, coming toward the bed.

"I only came to look after you while you were laid up," Sharon reminded him, her voice cool as she folded the blouse, laid it beside the first, and picked up the next one. "You're on your feet. You don't need me anymore, so there isn't any reason for me to stay, is there?"

She made a project out of buttoning the blouse, waiting for his response to her faintly challenging question, even at this stage hoping against hope that he would express regret to see her go.

"No, I guess there isn't," Ridge agreed easily, and frissons of pain broke over her nerves.

"Then there's nothing left to be said, is there?" she said tightly and pushed the half-folded blouse on top of the others in a short burst of raw impatience.

When she reached for the pair of jeans, she suddenly felt his hand under her chin, turning it so he could see her face. Except for that one brief glance when he'd entered, Sharon had kept her head averted, never looking directly at him. She quickly jerked her head away, but not before his alert gaze had swept the tautened skin around her eyes and the drained look of her complexion. She braced herself for some comment, but none came. Nor was there another attempt to inspect her face.

"As soon as I'm packed, I'll call home and have someone come pick me up," Sharon said into the silence.

"There's no need to have someone make a special trip over here to get you. I'll have one of the men drive you home," Ridge stated, showing that his arrangements were final by turning and leaving the room.

Alone again, Sharon pressed the jeans against her quivering chin. There had been no arguments, no protests, no regrets from Ridge, only a calm acceptance of the news that she was leaving. She asked herself what she had expected, but there wasn't any answer to that now.

When she finished packing, she discovered Ridge had left the house. She glanced out the kitchen window and saw him standing with Hobbs and another cowboy beside one of the ranch's pickups. With a touch of grim wryness, Sharon realized he'd wasted no time carrying out her transportation arrangements.

She left the house by the back door, carrying her suitcase, and crossed the yard to join the men standing by the truck's cab. She was painfully conscious of Ridge's gaze watching her all the way, its shuttered look never altering under the hat pulled low on his forehead.

"Have you got everything?" Ridge took the suitcase from her and passed it to the cowboy to be stowed in the bed of the truck.

"Yes." Everything that was hers to take.

His steady gaze was leveled at her, not allowing her to look away. "Thanks for coming."

A flash of bitter and taunting mockery broke across her tautly held features. "It was the neighborly thing to do." There was a twist in the smiling curve of her mouth.

Sharon swung away and climbed into the passenger side of the pickup. Ridge stepped away from it as the motor turned over and revved to life. Before the truck pulled away, he had already turned and begun talking to his foreman. Her eyes were painfully dry as Sharon stared out the front windshield.

# Chapter Ten

"Okay, Huck, now it's your turn." Sharon looped the reins around the chestnut's neck and made sure the hackamore was properly adjusted roughly three fingers above the flaring nostrils before she swung into the saddle.

The sleek gelding stood quietly, waiting for the command to move away from the fence where the bay filly stood tied, finished with her morning training session. A faintly satisfied smile touched Sharon's mouth as she walked the chestnut into the dirt corral. With six horses contracted to break and train, she usually split them into two groups, working one in the morning and the other in the cool of late afternoon. The spoiled and unruly chestnut was an exception, the only horse she worked morning and night. Two weeks of that steady routine were showing results, even if they hadn't changed the horse's mischievous personality.

Her opinion of the animal's worth was slowly being revised—upward. She put the chestnut through his paces—walk, trot, canter, change leads, round turns—until she was satisfied the horse was working nicely and responding well to the pressure of the hackamore.

Bringing the horse down to a walk, she reached forward and patted the sleek neck under the flaxen mane. "I think you're ready to start learning a 'fancy whoa,' Huck," she said and watched the horse's ears swivel back to catch the sound of her soft voice.

The fancy whoa was the sliding stop where the horse seems to sit on its haunches and screw its tail into the ground. Sharon changed her grip on the reins, taking one in each hand in a "squaw's hold." She lifted the chestnut into a slow jog and waited until he was relaxed in the gait, then squeezed lightly with her legs to urge his hindquarters forward. At the same time, she applied slight pressure with the left rein. The instant the chestnut began to respond, she slacked off the left rein and tightened the right rein, then continued alternating the pressure. She sensed the horse's confusion as it came to a slightly jerky stop.

After reassuring the gelding with a few soft-spoken words, Sharon put him into a trot again and repeated the procedure. It didn't take too many times before the chestnut started to lower its rump the minute he felt the leg pressure. She gave him time to balance himself before she checked his head.

There was a strong sense of accomplishment in

knowing the chestnut had stopped challenging her authority and struggling stubbornly to have his own way, and had begun to enjoy learning. More than the other green horses, Huck had given a purpose to these last two weeks since she'd left Latigo. Except when she worked the horses, Sharon lived in an emotionless void, one day sliding into another, the dull ache inside always with her.

As she debated whether to test the chestnut's response at a lope or to wait until the evening session for the next step, Sharon heard the pickup truck drive into the ranch yard. Absently her glance swung around to identify the visitor. A queer sense of panic rushed through her nerves when she recognized Ridge climbing out of the cab. She jerked her gaze to the front and struggled to calm the leaping of her pulse. It was the first time she'd seen Ridge since leaving his ranch that Sunday morning.

All over again, she had to come to terms with these occasional meetings that were bound to occur as long as they lived on neighboring ranches. After overcoming her teenage infatuation with him once already, it didn't seem fair that she had to go through this anguish again. Sharon kept consoling herself with the knowledge that she had succeeded once, so she could do it again.

As the chestnut circled the corral at a jogging trot, she saw Ridge approach the fence instead of going to the house. He moved with loose-limbed ease, obviously recovered from his stiffness. She jammed her hat further down on her forehead and lifted the gelding into a canter.

Tension ripped through her nerves when Ridge climbed the fence and sat on the top rail to watch her working the horse. Sharon wanted to scream in frustration. The blaze-faced chestnut was sensitive to the change in mood and began acting up, breaking stride and dancing skittishly around a turn.

Irritated with herself, Sharon slowed the gelding to a walk, trying to settle him down. The horse did a side-stepping jig, refusing to stride out cleanly, and tossed his head. She reined him to a stop, but the chestnut wouldn't stand still, moving nervously beneath her.

It was a lost cause, she realized. The horse was picking up her tension and agitation. It was pointless to fight the chestnut and risk souring his training to this level. As she gave up and walked the horse toward the fence where the bay filly was tied, she noticed her mother was standing at the fence with Ridge. Sharon avoided his eyes.

"Are you quitting?" her mother asked. Then she commented sympathetically, "He was working so well."

"I've pushed him a lot lately," Sharon replied, as if that explained the chestnut's actions this morning.

Ridge vaulted lightly to the ground and walked to the chestnut's head, catching hold of the bridle and rubbing its nose while Sharon dismounted.

Without looking at him, she hooked a stirrup on the saddlehorn and began loosening the cinch.

"He isn't even warm," Ridge observed, running a hand down the horse's chest.

"I ride him morning and night so I don't work him 'til he's hot," Sharon explained shortly. "I don't want him going stale on me when he's still learning."

She was stiff with tension, all her muscles tightly coiled and her nerves on edge. There was an electricity in the air, crackling in the stillness broken only by the idle stomping of a hoof and groaning of saddle leather.

Her mother came forward. "There's fresh coffee at the house. Would you like a cup, Ridge?"

"Not now, thanks," he refused. "I'll give Sharon a hand with the horses." Turning, he untied the filly's reins and prepared to lead her to the barn.

"I can manage without any help," she insisted, feeling brittle and breakable.

"I know it," he replied easily and calmly. "But I want to talk to you."

Sharon flashed an anguished look at her mother, but her only response was a pair of raised eyebrows and a faint smile. If Ridge was determined to talk to Sharon, nothing would stop him. Her mother knew that. Gritting her teeth, Sharon scooped up the chestnut's reins and headed for the barn.

The barn was full of hay dust and horse smells, shadowed and cool, as Sharon led the chestnut into his stall and clipped on his halter before removing the hackamore. Ridge led the filly into the adjoining stall and began unsaddling her, working in silence.

Unbuckling the double cinch, Sharon hauled the saddle off the chestnut and swung it onto her hip. She scooped the saddle blanket and pad off the horse's back and headed for the tack room with her double burden. Ridge followed her, not seeming to pay any attention when she stole a glance at him. The saddles were heaved onto their racks and the blankets and pads draped over them to air out the horse sweat.

The continued silence grated on her nerves as they returned to the respective stalls of their horses. Sharon picked up a currycomb and began brushing down the sleek chestnut while it nosed at the manger full of hay. Her jaw was clenched so tightly shut that her teeth hurt.

"You wanted to talk to me," she finally challenged Ridge, without breaking the rhythm of her brushing strokes.

"Yeah." The sweep of a second currycomb filled the pause that accompanied his bland acknowledgement. Sharon waited, the moment stretching out. Almost idly, Ridge said, "Those wildflowers you picked finally died. I threw them out yesterday."

"I'm surprised they lasted so long." She couldn't seem to keep the curtness out of her voice.

"So was I," he replied.

There was another interminably long silence. Sharon finally threw him a tight-lipped glance over the back of the chestnut. "Is that what you wanted to tell me?"

He stopped abruptly and rested his arms on the filly's dark back, the currycomb hanging loosely from his fingers. His head was tipped to the side, his rolled hat brim at an angle that shaded his expression. He swore softly under his breath and pushed away from the horse, his hard gaze boring into hers.

"I've come to accept your terms," Ridge stated.

"My terms?" Her mouth stayed slightly open. In puzzled confusion, she watched him walk around the horse and come to the corner of the stall where she was standing.

"Yes, your terms," he repeated and reached into his bulging shirt pocket.

Instead of taking out a cigarette as Sharon expected, he removed a small square box and stepped forward to push it into her hand. She stared at the ring box, then hesitantly opened it, darting him a wary look. His features remained cut in stern lines.

A pear-shaped diamond sparkled in its mounting on a narrow, gold band. A raw joy flamed through her, but Sharon was afraid to believe in it. She lifted her gaze and searched his face.

"Why are you giving me this?" There was a trace of hoarseness in her low-worded question.

His blue glance flicked at the ring then back to her. "You said that's what you wanted," he reminded her with a certain flatness. "I can't get you the marriage license until we get blood tests. And we'll have to work on the kids you wanted." She felt the pinning thrust of his gaze. "I believe those were the three things you said you wanted—in that order."

Her fingers gripped the small jewelry box, a tremor of pain running through her. That was what she had said she wanted, but foolishly, she had left out love. She was angry and hurt, somehow feeling insulted.

"Well?" Ridge prompted roughly.

The hurt blazed in her hazel eyes. "This has to be the most unromantic proposal I've heard in my life!" she retorted, snapping the box shut and ramming it into his hand as she pushed her way by him.

But Ridge was no longer hampered by his injuries. His hand grabbed her arm before she had taken two strides away from him and spun her back around. Impatience and irritation flared in his eyes.

"What do you expect me to do?" he demanded. "Get down on one knee and beg for your hand in marriage?"

"That would be equally laughable!" She pulled her arm free of his hand with an angry yank and turned again.

"Sharon." There was an ache in the way he said her name that made Sharon pause. His hands moved onto the back of her shoulders, trembling slightly as they touched her. All her senses strained to search out this difference. "I want you to come home with me—back to Latigo."

A warmth was spreading from his hands as Ridge

moved closer. Sharon was afraid that his physical influence would somehow undermine her control. She swung around to face him and pressed her back against the rough boards of the barn wall partition, flattening her hands against it, too, while she eyed him with wary hope.

"Why?" she asked tightly.

He moved in, bracing his hands against the wall on either side of her, effectively trapping her. The intensity of his gaze unnerved her as he leaned closer, tipping his head down, which made it seem nearer to her face. She felt enveloped by his closeness, a captive of his tough and rugged male vigor.

"It never bothered me to walk into an empty house before," he said. "But I can't get used to you not being there. Every time I walk into the kitchen, I expect to see you. In the mornings when I wake up, I listen for the sounds of you stirring somewhere in the house. You didn't take everything when you left," he accused. "Your ghost is there, haunting me with the way it was."

"You'll get over it in time," she suggested huskily.

"That's what I've been telling myself for the last two weeks," Ridge agreed. "That's what I said yesterday when I threw those dead flowers out. But I could still smell them in the room—the same way I could still smell you."

His head dipped closer as if inhaling her scent. Her lashes fluttered, nearly closing at the rush of exquisite pain his reply brought. But she had gone through too much heartache to be so easily swayed by him.

"God knows I tried not to think about you," he said huskily. "You'll never know how hard I tried."

"Then why did you?" Her voice was turning into a whisper, the look in his eye beginning to melt her weakening resistance.

"I was satisfied with my life the way it was before you came. I thought I'd be content with it again after you left. But you don't really miss something until it isn't there. There's a void where you were, and I want you to come back and fill it."

"Why?" She kept asking the same question in a different phrasing, trying to get him to say the answer she wanted to hear.

"Because I miss you." His mouth was almost against her cheek, his breath spilling warmly over her skin. Their hat brims were rubbing against each other, but it was the only contact, although she could almost feel the sensation of his mouth moving to form the words he spoke. "I want you to come home with me, but I know how stubborn you can be. I knew you wouldn't agree unless it was on your terms."

"That's why you bought the ring?" Sharon breathed the question, feeling so boneless that she needed the barn wall for support. Inside she was a quivering mass of emotion, barely held in check.

"Yes." He was in front of her mouth, hovering close to her lips. "Will you come with me now?"

"It won't work, Ridge." It cost her a lot to deny

herself the kiss he was offering. "Not unless it's what you want, too."

"I want you. Hell, I need you," Ridge muttered thickly. "I'll take you any way I can have you. And if that means marrying you, then we'll get married."

"Are you sure it's what you want?" she insisted because his answer had been far from reassuring on that score.

"I'm damned sure *you* are what I want." His mouth closed onto her lips, burning into them with hunger.

Her hands went to his waist as he gathered her away from the wall and pulled her into his arms. He crushed her to his length, unable to get enough of her as he strained to absorb her whole. It was a spinning world, a carousel ride, and she had the brass ring within her reach.

The crushing band of his arms had lifted her onto her toes while the driving force of his kiss arched her backwards. Her hat was swept off her head and sailed to a pile of straw in the corner. Sharon reeled under the desperate urgency of his kiss, which revealed a hint of vulnerability that gave her renewed hope.

When he dragged his mouth from hers, a hand cupped the back of her head and pressed it to his shoulder as if he didn't want her to see what was written in his face. Sharon felt the shudder that went through him. There was a soaring lift of her heart in reaction.

"Ridge, it doesn't have to be all on my terms," she said, listening to the wild run of his heartbeat. "I do want children, but—what about you?"

A short laugh became mixed up in the roughness of his breath. His hand relaxed its pressure on her head, letting her draw away from his shoulder to look up at him. A fiery satisfaction burned blue-bright in his eyes.

"Shall I be honest?" he asked with a quirk of one brow.

"Yes." Never in her life had she wanted him to be more honest about something than now.

"I keep remembering how you looked that day with that little boy riding on your hip while you tried to chase those loose horses back into the corral—and I remembered how it was in the kitchen that day . . . you baking cookies while little Tony and I ate them." His gaze moved randomly over her upturned face, memorizing its features. "I think about that and imagine what it would be like if that was our son and all the things I could show him. I might like it better if we had a girl, though." His callus-roughened hand stroked the tawny silk of her hair while he studied its color and texture. "A little girl with toffee-colored hair who would sit on my lap and tell me about the boys who teased her in school and pulled her braids."

"You mean that, don't you?" Sharon realized with breathless wonder.

"Yes." His gaze smoldered on her face once more. He drew back, their hips keeping contact while he ran his hand down the valley between her breasts and came to a stop on her flat stomach. "I'm looking forward to this little stomach of yours growing round with our child. I want it, whatever sex it turns out to be. But—" Ridge paused "—there's two things that have to come before it."

She was so enthralled with the discovery that he wanted a family—that he wanted *their* family—she didn't follow his meaning. "What two things?"

"First is the ring, if I haven't lost it." He felt in his side pocket where he'd shoved it for safekeeping when she'd thrust it into his hand and started to leave. This time, he took the diamond ring out of the box and slipped it on her trembling finger.

It seemed to wink at her, as if it knew a wonderful secret. Happiness was tumbling from her, crystal bright and clear like the cascading waters of a Colorado stream running swift and pure.

Her heart was in her eyes when she looked at him, then she threw her arms around his neck and kissed him with all the pent-up emotion of those long years. She clung to him fiercely, openly showing him how much she cared, until the frustration of holding it back for so long was spent.

"I love you so much it hurts," she declared and hugged him tightly.

"The way I am?" There was an earnestness in his demand.

Sharon set back on her heels and gazed at him, a smile beaming. "The way you are—no pedestal and no shining armor. I love the grumbler that snaps when he's irritable. I love the tough cowboy that doesn't want anyone to see he's hurt—"

"Except you. You wouldn't let me hide the pain from you," he remembered.

"I don't want a hero, Ridge," she assured him. "I just want the man I love. I don't want you to be anything but what you are. When you're hurt, I want to know it. And when you're happy, I want to be happy with you. That's all."

"Maybe if you had seen me like this a long time ago, I would have forgotten sooner that my best friend was your brother," he mused idely. "It's funny. Now I think of him as being your brother, instead of you being his sister. Sharon, what have you done to me?"

"I haven't done anything to you."

"Haven't you?" Ridge mocked. "You've put me through a wringer and taken the starch out of me. I think Scott is convinced that bull did more than stomp me."

"Scott? Why?" Sharon couldn't recall her brother saying a word to her about Ridge's behavior. Of course, every time Ridge's name had been mentioned in her presence lately, she'd left the room.

"Because of the way I grilled him the other night about that Rivers fella. It was all I could talk about—all I could think about," he admitted. "Scott didn't improve the situation either with his constant chuckling."

"You said you weren't jealous." She eyed him, beginning to doubt his disclaimer.

"I wasn't," he denied, then lifted a shoulder in a reluctant shrug. "Maybe I was. I know I was mad clean through."

"Why?" Sharon questioned, studying him more closely with a speculating gleam in her look.

"Because you were wearing that dress," Ridge admitted, a trace of a vaguely chagrined smile showing at the corners of his mouth. "You had it on that day you brought me home from the hospital. I guess I thought of it as 'my' dress. I can't explain it. But when I saw you wearing it to go out on a date with another guy, I felt betrayed somehow."

"It was all I had to wear except jeans."

"You didn't have to go out with him," he reminded her grimly. "You were supposed to be taking care of me, not gallivanting all over the countryside."

"You seemed well enough to manage on your own for one evening," Sharon murmured.

"I was. As a matter of fact, I think subconsciously I took my time about getting better. I liked having you around, and it was one way to keep you there longer."

"When I told you I was leaving, you didn't put up any fuss," she remembered. "I had the feeling you were glad to see me go."

"That's because when you left, I thought things would go back on an even keel. And I also knew if you stayed, I'd end up making love to you—by fair means or foul," he sighed briefly. "I knew I'd have trouble looking you—or your family—in the eye if I had taken advantage of the situation. Mainly, though, I realized I couldn't do that to you when I heard you crying in your room. I didn't want to hurt you again."

"You heard me?" Sharon frowned. "But the radio—"

"I turned it on. You have your pride, too, and I thought you'd rather I didn't know you were crying." His finger touched her cheek as if seeking traces of those tears. "I didn't know it could hurt me so much to hear someone else's sobbing."

"I only cried because I loved you so much. I knew I had to leave and I didn't want to go," she explained.

"Now you can come back to stay."

"Are you sure you won't get tired of having me around all the time?" she asked, melting against him as his arms tightened in possession.

"You never get tired of having people around that you love," Ridge chided and didn't understand her choked cry of elation, because he'd finally said the word she'd been longing to hear, but he understood the outpouring of desire in her kiss.

# JANET DAILEY

## America's Bestselling Romance Novelist

Read these wonderful stories and experience the magic that
has made Janet Dailey a star in the world of books.

- ☐ THE GREAT ALONE ...................................87504-3/$6.99
- ☐ THE PRIDE OF HANNAH WADE .................87510-8/$5.99
- ☐ THE GLORY GAME ....................................87503-5/$5.99
- ☐ THE SECOND TIME ...................................87513-2/$4.99
- ☐ SILVER WINGS, SANTIAGO BLUE .............87515-9/$6.50
- ☐ THE BEST WAY TO LOSE ...........................87499-3/$5.99
- ☐ WESTERN MAN .........................................87521-3/$5.99
- ☐ FOXFIRE LIGHT .........................................87502-7/$5.99
- ☐ SEPARATE CABINS ...................................87514-0/$4.99
- ☐ TERMS OF SURRENDER .............................87519-1/$5.99
- ☐ FOR THE LOVE OF GOD .............................87501-9/$6.50
- ☐ THE LANCASTER MEN ...............................87506-X/$4.99
- ☐ HOSTAGE BRIDE .......................................87505-1/$4.99
- ☐ NIGHTWAY ...............................................87509-4/$6.99
- ☐ RIDE THE THUNDER ...................................87511-6/$5.99
- ☐ THE ROGUE ..............................................87512-4/$5.99
- ☐ TOUCH THE WIND .....................................87520-5/$5.99
- ☐ THIS CALDER SKY .....................................87518-3/$6.99
- ☐ THIS CALDER RANGE .................................87517-5/$5.99
- ☐ STANDS A CALDER MAN .............................87516-7/$6.99
- ☐ CALDER BORN, CALDER BRED ..........87500-0/$6.99
- ☐ LEFTOVER LOVE ..............................87507-8/$6.99
- ☐ MISTLETOE AND HOLLY ....................87508-6/$4.99

**POCKET BOOKS**

# JUDE DEVERAUX

*America's favorite historical romance author!*

Join the *New York Times* bestselling author as she transports us from modern-day Virginia to the high mountain deserts of 1873 Colorado, with a vibrant new tale about a feisty lady and the man she was meant to love.

# LEGEND

Available in hardcover
from Pocket Books

POCKET
B O O K S

1273-01

# JULIE GARWOOD

Ten *New York Times* bestsellers—
including her latest, *For the Roses*—
verify what Julie Garwood's fans
have always know: she is a master-
ful storyteller. "Julie Garwood
attracts readers like beautiful hero-
ines attract dashing heroes," says
USA *Today*. Now, returning to the
enchanting world she created in
*The Bride*, she delights us again
with another fascinating tale of love,
adventure, and soaring ambitions,
set in twelfth-century Scotland....

## The Wedding

Available in Hardcover
from Pocket Books

POCKET
**B O O K S**

1196-01